'You need an heiress,' Harry heard his brother say in his mind. An heiress would indeed be an answer for Hilltop. And he himself would admit that companionship, a partner, would be most welcome.

Harry looked down at Helen—at her brilliant smile, the flash of jewels in her hair—and for an instant felt the tug of temptation towards a life that had never been his. A life of carefree glitter.

And then, over the swirl of the dancers, he glimpsed Rose Parker, laughing with the other musicians as her slender fingers skipped lightly over the keys. And he was drawn towards her soft warmth that was like a fire on a cold day, sustaining and sweet.

But Rose deserved far more than he had to offer—a wounded soldier whose house was falling down around him. That was one thing he did know for sure.

Author Note

When I was a child, my grandmother loved Christmas! I loved visiting her house at that time of year, because she had a huge tree covered with sparkling glass ornaments, dishes full of candy and a pair of beautiful antique Santa and Mrs Santa dolls, which sat high on a shelf because I was allowed to look but not to play with them. Now they belong to me I still don't play with them, afraid she might be watching from on high! I think she inherited this love of Christmas from her own grandmother, who grew up at the end of that heyday of Christmas: the Victorian Age.

The people of the Regency era weren't quite as elaborate in their celebration of Christmas as those of the Victorian age, but they did have a fun-filled family holiday. Even though there weren't large evergreen trees there was greenery: holly, ivy, rosemary, and mistletoe boughs that are very useful for romance authors. On Christmas Day, there might be small gifts—books, handkerchiefs, maybe toys for the children—a walk to church and then a large, merry dinner, with roasted goose, mincemeat pies and puddings, followed by games like Bob Apple and Snapdragon. On Boxing Day the servants would be given their gifts and maybe some time off to visit their own families.

I loved getting to spend time in a Regency Christmas, and to remember some of my own childhood traditions, too! If you'd like more of a peek behind the history, please visit my website at ammandamccabe.com.

THE
WALLFLOWER'S
MISTLETOE
WEDDING

Amanda McCabe

Published in Great Britain 2017
by Mills & Boon, an imprint of HarperCollins*Publishers*
1 London Bridge Street, London, SE1 9GF

© 2017 Ammanda McCabe

ISBN: 978-0-263-92615-6

Printed and bound in Spain
by CPI, Barcelona

Amanda McCabe wrote her first romance at the age of sixteen—a vast epic, starring all her friends as the characters, written secretly during algebra class. She's never since used algebra, but her books have been nominated for many awards, including the RITA®, Romantic Times Reviewers' Choice Award, the Booksellers' Best, the National Readers' Choice Award, and the Holt Medallion. She lives in Oklahoma with her husband, one dog and one cat.

Visit the Author Profile page
at millsandboon.co.uk for more titles.

To the memory of my grandmother, Roberta McCabe, who loved the magic of Christmas.

Prologue

Barton Park—summer 1820

'Oh, Rose! Doesn't the music just make you want to twirl and twirl and twirl?'

Rose Parker sat back on her heels and laughed as she watched her sister, Lily, spin in an exuberant circle, her new white lace and tulle skirts like a great cloud. The music from the party floated up to their chamber and it was indeed very twirly. 'You won't twirl for long if I don't finish that hem. It will come unravelled and you will trip and fall flat on your face—right in front of Mr Hewlitt.'

Lily came to an abrupt stop, stumbling on her satin slippers. 'Oh, no, Rose!' she cried, her pretty, heart-shaped face full of stark fear.

'I could never do such a thing. How he would despise me!'

Rose laughed again. She couldn't help it; her sister's adorable ways were always too funny. 'Lily, my dearest, Mr Hewlitt would never in a thousand years despise you for anything. In fact, stumbling and falling into his arms would probably only make him worship you more as his delicate angel.'

A tiny smile broke through Lily's pout. 'I—well, perhaps so. He is so terribly sweet.'

'And terribly sweet on you. Mama says he will surely ask you something very important indeed tonight,' Rose said. She did have to tease Lily just a bit, as she always had, even when her sister was a tiny, golden-curled cherub prone to blushing and shrieking when provoked. But she was serious, too. Mr Hewlitt had been stammering his way up to just such a moment for weeks and this ball at their cousins' home at Barton Park to celebrate midsummer seemed the perfect opportunity. It was true that he was a curate with only a middling income, yet everyone could see how good he was at his calling, so caring and energetic. Surely a bishopric waited for him one day!

And he adored Lily, as she did him. Together the two of them were as adorable as a box of new puppies.

Rose was happy for her sister, yet wistful, too. With just herself and their mother, their cottage would be much too quiet. Too lonely.

Rose sighed. She would have to procure a kitten, or mayhap a songbird. Wasn't that what useful spinsters did? Collect pets, especially cats, and knit them little sweaters and such? It sounded rather diverting.

'Come, dearest Lily, let me finish the hem,' she said. 'Or the dancing will be over before Mr Hewlitt can find you.'

Lily climbed back on to the low stool, watching in the mirror with a little frown as Rose plied her needle through the delicate beaded tulle. 'Do you really, truly think he will propose?'

'Of course he will.'

'Do—do you think I should accept, then? Right away?'

Rose was surprised at her sister's suddenly unsure, quiet tone. She glanced up to see that

Lily did indeed look worried, something most uncharacteristic. She quickly thought back on Mr Hewlitt's courtship: his visits to the cottage, his little gifts of bouquets and books of poetry, his walks with Lily, the way they stared at each other as if there was no one else around at all. Had she missed something? 'Do you have doubts, dearest? Has he done something—ungentlemanly?' She couldn't quite imagine that, but then again one never really knew with men. Look how their own father had concealed his debts, his terrible gambling habits, from his wife and daughters until he died and they were cast out of their home.

Surely Mr Hewlitt would never do that. If he dared to hurt Lily in any way, Rose would murder him.

'Oh, no, not at all! It's just—' Lily broke off, biting her lip. 'Well, what will you and Mama do?'

'Oh, Lily.' Rose gave her the most reassuring smile she could manage. Was that not the very same question she had asked herself since Father died? 'You must not worry about that, dearest. We will be absolutely fine. Indeed, I'm quite looking forward to making your chamber into my very own sitting room. The mind reels at the thought of so much space! I will be just like a duchess with my own suite.'

Lily laughed, as well she would. Their cottage was approximately the size of a thimble, even with Lily's extra little chamber they had built at the back. 'And you will visit me very often, won't you? I won't be far away.'

'So often you will be heartily sick of me.'

'Promise?'

'Just try to keep me away.' Rose finished the last stitch in the hem and stood up to give her sister a hug, careful not to muss her ruffles and curls. Lily smelled of violet powder and sweetness, just as she had when she was a child, and Rose had held her dimpled little hands to help her walk. She laughed to keep from crying.

'You really should marry first, as the eldest daughter. That is the natural way,' Lily said.

Rose laughed again. 'Find me another Mr Hewlitt, then. Until I have just such a paragon, I would never be able to tolerate wifely duties.'

'He *is* out there, Rose, I just know it! The perfect man for you.' Lily drew back to stare most earnestly into Rose's eyes. 'You will find him when you least expect it, just as I did with Mr Hewlitt.'

'I haven't time for romance,' Rose said, tucking away her needle and thread in her workbox. It was quite true. When their father died so suddenly and they had to leave their home for the cottage, they'd had a very small income that would keep them from starving, but there would be no carriage or smart clothes or abundance of servants. Rose herself did much of the work: sweeping, sewing, looking after the chickens, taking care of their frail mother. She didn't mind very much; she actually quite liked the useful, busy feeling of tea to make and ironing of petticoats to finish. And her chickens were known to be the finest layers in the neighbourhood.

Their mother, however, *did* mind. Mrs Felicity Parker had grown up as gentry in a fine manor house, cousin to the ancient family of the Bancrofts of Barton Park, and expected more of the same from her marriage, only to be bitterly disappointed. She talked of it to anyone who would listen. All her hopes had long been pinned on the beautiful Lily marrying well. A poor curate had never been in her plans, no matter how kind and handsome he was, no matter how much he adored Lily. And Rose saw too clearly what happened when a woman had to trust in marriage, trust in a man. She wasn't sure she could do it.

Rose sighed. She very much feared her mother's plans might turn to herself now and this visit to Barton Park was part of them. As much as she enjoyed seeing the old house and meeting her cousins, she couldn't let her guard down.

'Are you quite well, Rose?' Lily asked, frowning in concern. 'You look as if you have the headache.'

Rose made herself smile and fluffed up the lace trim of her sister's sleeve. 'Not at all. It's just a bit stuffy in here, don't you think? We should make our way down to the party. Mr Hewlitt will surely arrive soon.'

With a squeal of excitement, Lily dashed out of the room, her gown floating and sparkling around her like angel's wings. Rose took a quick glance at herself in the glass before she followed, to make sure she looked presentable and tidy.

Presentable and *tidy* were about all she could hope for, she thought wryly. Unlike Lily, she had not inherited their mother's blond curls and pink cheeks, her petite plumpness. Rose was taller, thin to the point of sharpness, with light brown hair that refused to hold a curl no matter how long it was subjected to the tongs, and skin that had turned ever so slightly golden while working in the garden. Her eyes were not too bad, she thought, with a small spark of hopefulness. A green-hazel that looked emerald in some lights, when she did not have to wear the horrid spectacles. Sadly, those had become more and more necessary of late, especially when sitting up sewing in the lamplight.

She smoothed the sleeves of her gown and reached for her gloves. Unlike Lily's new dress, Rose had redone an old gown of their mother's for herself. The olive-gold satin, plain and lustrous with only a single row of gold embroidery at the hem, suited her much better than the current style for frothy pale muslins and ruffled sleeves, and her needle had managed to take in the fuller skirts and puff out the sleeves a bit, yet she feared it would attract whispers of 'unfashionableness' and pity for the poor Parkers.

'Ah, well,' she told herself. 'Fashion is something you could never really aspire to, Rose dear.'

She laughed, straightened the ivory comb in her upswept hair, slid her creamy Indian shawl over her shoulders and followed Lily out the door.

The party downstairs was just beginning, the first arrivals sweeping through the front doors and gathering in the marble-floored hall, leaving their wraps with the footmen, calling out merry greetings to each other.

Rose peeked over the gilded banister to the scene below. She had always loved Barton Park, the home of her mother's distant cousins, the Bancrofts, even though they so seldom got to visit. It was a beautiful house, not too small and not too grand, built on elegant, classic lines and filled with comfortable furnishings and plenty of books and art. A true family home for many generations, soaked through with stories and emotions and hopes. It had fallen into some disrepair for a few years, but under the care of the current owners, Jane, Countess of Ramsay, and her sister, Emma, it had found new life.

The gardens beyond the tall glass windows were equally lovely, especially on such a soft, warm summer's evening. Chinese lanterns shimmered in the trees, lighting up the pathways and the colourful tumble of the flowerbeds as carriages bounced along the gravel drive to the waiting doors.

Rose studied the crowd, a laughing, beautifully dressed throng gathered around Jane and her husband, the magnificently handsome Lord Ramsay. Jane looked as if she had belonged there at Barton Park for ever in her elegant dark blue gown, shimmering with lavender beads. She greeted each new arrival with a happy cry, sparkling with laughter before she passed them to her younger sister, Emma, a blonde angel much like Lily in her grey satin gown. Emma, too, smiled, though it was quieter, more unsure. When they were children, Emma had been quite the daredevil, but now she had returned to Barton as a young widow, trailing something of a scandal in her wake. Rose quite adored her, even as she worried for her.

The growing throng appeared a bit of a blur to Rose without her spectacles, but she glimpsed Lily near the open doors to the drawing room, where the music was drifting out above the hum of laughter. Their mother stood beside her, the plumes of her striped turban nodding merrily as she laughed and chattered, but Lily didn't seem to be paying attention at all. She bounced on the toes of her dancing slippers, searching each face around her eagerly before falling back again.

Oh, dear, Rose thought. Mr Hewlitt had probably not made his appearance yet. She tiptoed down the stairs and slipped into the crowd, intending to make her way to Lily and their mother. She was stopped when Jane spotted her.

'Rose, my dear, do come and meet someone!' Jane said, grasping Rose's hand and drawing her forward. Jane was the kindest of women, but always most assiduous in her hostess duties. She would never just let a wallflower be a wallflower.

Rose flashed a quick smile at Emma, who smiled back uncomfortably. She looked as if she wanted to run for the safety of the comfortably shabby library as much as Rose did.

But then Rose turned to face Jane's newly arrived guests—and froze. All thoughts of fleeing, all thoughts at all, were quite gone.

A gentleman had just stepped through the front door and what a gentleman he was. He looked rather like something Rose would picture in one of the romantic French novels Lily liked to read aloud in the evenings—a man tall, dark and mysterious. His expression was quite solemn and wary as he studied the crowd, as if he was thinking of possible battle lines rather than dancing.

He certainly did have the bearing of a soldier, lean and ramrod-straight, his shoulders strong beneath the cut of his dark blue evening coat, his sun-darkened skin set off by a plain white cravat. His hair, so dark it was almost a blue-black, like a winter's night, waved back from his forehead, and his eyes were a velvet brown. He had a strange stillness, a perfect watchfulness, almost a—a menace about him, but one that was entic-

ing rather than frightening. He was quite unlike anyone else she had ever seen.

'Harry, how delightful you could come tonight after all,' Jane was saying, once Rose
could tear her attention away from the man's
mesmerising handsomeness and hear the roar
of the party again. 'We did hear you were off
to battle in Sicily.'

'A soldier has to keep busy however he
can.' The man smiled as he bowed over Jane's
hand and it quite transformed him. He went
from wary stillness to sunny charm in an instant, a dimple appearing in his sun-browned
cheek that made Rose want to giggle like a
schoolgirl. 'But it seems they don't need my
assistance at this very moment. How could I
resist the chance to see *you* again, Lady Ramsay? It's been much too long since you brightened the dull London ballrooms. Hayden is
a beast to keep you away.'

Jane laughed and waved her lace fan at
him. 'Silly flatterer. I know you are merely
counting the seconds until you can escape to
the library for a brandy with Hayden and a
talk about your beastly battlefields. But it's
lovely to see you again all the same, safe and

sound. And you, Charles! Where on earth have you been keeping yourself?'

Rose was able to tear her gaze from the dark, poetic brooder for a moment to see another man standing just behind him. He was also tall, also handsome, with a cheerful smile and bright golden hair, and the same brown eyes as the first man. But though he was just as good looking, he did not have the same frightening magnetism.

'Nowhere as useful as my brother, I assure you, Lady Ramsay,' he said with a bow. 'But I haven't had a proper dance in ages and, unlike Harry, I miss it more than I can say.'

'That is one thing I can promise here. I hired the best orchestra from miles around.' Jane drew Rose and Emma forward. 'Emma, Rose, may I present two of our neighbours? Captain Henry St George, who was a great hero at Waterloo, and his brother, Mr Charles St George. Gentlemen, this my sister, Mrs Emma Carrington, and my cousin Miss Rose Parker.'

Charles was the first to bow to them, with grand courtly flourishes that made Rose laugh and even had Emma smiling. 'Ladies,

I fear that unlike my dashing brother I am hero of very little except the billiards room, but I do claim some proficiency at waltzing, if you will do me the honour?'

Emma did laugh—the first time Rose had heard it since the young widow had returned to Barton—but Rose could still not find a way to tear her attention completely away from Captain St George. How very intriguing he looked, with his wry flash of a smile!

'Do you live near Barton, Miss Parker?' he asked, his voice low and deep, almost rough. He watched her closely, as if he listened only to her in the whole room.

'Oh,' Rose answered, and for an instant it was as if every word she had ever known flew out of her mind. She had to laugh at herself; it was quite unlike the sensible nature she usually prided herself on. Yet she comforted herself that no lady could surely be entirely immune from such a pair of eyes when they were focused so closely on oneself.

'Not too far,' she said. 'We used to visit often when we were children, my sister and I, and hunt for treasure with Jane and Emma.'

He smiled, his dark eyes crinkling at

the corners. 'Treasure? That does sound intriguing.'

'Oh, it was!' she said, absurdly pleased to have 'intrigued' him. She found she wanted more than anything to make him smile that smile at her again. 'It is a wonderful old tale, about the lover of a Royalist soldier, Arabella Bancroft, hiding a royal fortune on the grounds of the estate, in the hope she and her love would one day be reunited to spend it together. Or something like that. We were quite hazy on the details when we were children.'

'And did you ever find it?'

'No, not even a farthing. It's just a legend, of course, but we did have some marvellous adventures digging for it in the woods. We would climb the trees and pretend we were the Royalists defending our fortress from Cromwell, with tree trunks for cannons...' She suddenly remembered he was a true captain, a hero of the terrible carnage at Waterloo, and felt her cheeks turn warm. 'Not at all like real battle, of course.'

A shadow flickered over his smile and he glanced away. 'Much more fun, though, I would wager. Real battle is all mud and noise,

I fear, Miss Parker. But trees and branches as guns—just fun.'

Rose nervously twitched her skirts into place, feeling terrible at reminding him of such things when he was meant to be enjoying himself at Jane's party. Not for the first time, she wished she had some of Lily's gift of easy laughter and chatter. 'I am sure it was. I'm sorry for bringing up any bad memories, Captain.'

He gave her a wry smile. 'The memories are always there, Miss Parker, but they don't plague me on a night like this.' He paused to adjust a glove. 'And did they ever find each other again?'

'Find each other?' she said, confused.

'Arabella Bancroft and her Royalist.'

'Oh. No. He never came back. I think she married someone else in the end and abandoned Barton Park.'

'Then there is hope the treasure is still out there.'

'I never thought of it like that,' Rose exclaimed. 'Perhaps it is.'

Captain St George's brother suddenly turned towards them with a grin. 'Harry, I have just secured Mrs Carrington's promise for the first dance and Lady Ramsay tells me there are not yet enough couples for a proper set. You must find yourself a partner and do your bit for the party.'

'Charlie, you know I am hopeless dancer indeed,' the Captain protested.

'Of course you are not!' Charles said. 'Do not be an old stick in the mud again. Aren't you all about doing your duty? Well, being merry is your only duty tonight.'

Harry laughed, and turned back to Rose. 'Well, then, Miss Parker. Would you be brave enough to take me on for the first dance? With fair warning that grace is not my strong suit.'

Rose was not at all sure that could be true. He had such a lean, coiled stillness, she imagined that in motion he would be as elegant and lethal as a jungle cat. She longed to dance with him, more than she had ever longed for anything before, but she also feared he was asking only because she was the closest lady at the moment.

Not that it mattered. When would she ever be able to dance with such a man again?

'I—no, nor is it mine, Captain St George,' she answered. 'I do have a terrible tendency to trip over my own feet—my sister always hated sharing her dancing lessons with me. Perhaps we can figure it out together?'

He laughed and suddenly he looked so young, so carefree. Rose imagined perhaps he was like that all the time before he went to war and became so watchful. 'I am quite sure we can. The first dance, then, Miss Parker.'

'Yes, thank you, Captain,' she answered, and suddenly felt a hand on her arm. She turned to see Lily standing beside her, her sky-blue eyes wide.

'Oh, Rose!' she cried. 'He isn't here yet! What if he changed his mind?'

Before Rose could answer, the front doors flew open again as if in a stormy gale and a most fearsome figure appeared. As wide as she was tall, with iron-grey hair high-piled in the style of pre–Revolutionary France, and swathed in lace and satin, her dried-apple face was heavily rouged. Armed as she was with a carved walking stick with the head of a snarling dragon, she seemed the combination of Empress Maria Theresa and a Viking, combined with an ancient tree spirit.

'Aunt Sylvia,' Jane gasped. She hurried forward to try to help her, but the old lady impatiently pushed her away. 'How lovely to see you. We thought you could not attend tonight.'

Aunt Sylvia Pemberton. Rose stared at her in astonishment. She had thought the old lady, a sister of her own great-grandfather and Jane's and Emma's as well, was only some sort of legend, but now here she was before them. She lived in a vast house nearby, rich as Croesus and widowed for decades, but she never ventured beyond its gates. Even Captain St George seemed amazed by the sight, even after all he must have seen at Waterloo.

'I should never have ventured out indeed, Jane. A most disagreeable night and my rheumatism so terrible,' Aunt Sylvia growled. 'But I had to see what you have done with the old house, now that all your modern folderols have finished. You've quite ruined it, I must say. The windows are terrible and what kind of colour is that for walls?' She looked around, waving her stick as if the new pale blue paint was a personal affront.

'Ah,' she went on, 'and here is that disgraceful Emma, I see. And who is this? The Parker chits? How pale you are, girl. And the other one—too tall. Come here where I can see you better.'

Lily did indeed look quite white under such scrutiny and she clutched at Rose's hand. 'Must we?' Lily whispered.

Rose thought of the grandness of Aunt Sylvia's mansion and the tininess of their own cottage. She sighed. 'I think we must.' She glanced over her shoulder, but the Captain had quite vanished into the crowd. She could only fervently hope he remembered their dance.

'Don't worry, Lily dearest,' she whispered. 'We just have to say hello and then we can slip away. I am sure Mr Hewlitt will be here at any moment.'

'She might turn us into stone first,' Lily whispered back with a shiver.

Their mother suddenly appeared at Lily's other side, a smile on her face beneath the blond curls that peeked from her turban.

'Girls, be very nice indeed. We might need her help one day soon,' she hissed, before sailing forward to kiss Aunt Sylvia's cheek. 'Aunt Sylvia, how absolutely delightful to see you again after so long. You remember my dear daughters, Rose and Lily, I'm sure.'

'Hmmph,' Aunt Sylvia said with a thump of her stick. 'Still yours, are they? No husbands yet? How vexing for you, Felicity. I think we have much to talk about.'

As if he had been given a stage cue, Mr Hewlitt appeared in the doorway, looking handsome, but blushing and flustered in his curate's dark coat, his red hair rumpled. He lit up like the moon when he saw Lily, and hurried over to take her hand. 'Miss Parker, I am so sorry I was delayed! I have been so looking forward to—'

'And who are *you*, young man?' Aunt Sylvia boomed.

Poor Mr Hewlitt looked quite terrified, but much to his credit he did not let go of Lily's hand. Indeed, he slid in front of her, as if to protect her. 'I am Mr Peter Hewlitt, curate of St Anne's, madam.'

Rose took the opportunity to slip away

from the little scene and made her way through the crowd into the drawing room. The Aubusson rugs that usually lay over the polished parquet floors had been rolled away to make a dance floor, surrounded by conversational groupings of brocade sofas and armchairs, half-hidden by banks of palms and fragrant white flowers. The orchestra played on their dais, a soft song as dancers found their partners and footmen passed trays of champagne and claret punch. The windows were open to let in the soft summer breeze and everything was laughter and happiness for just a moment.

Rose smoothed her skirt again, hoping against hope Captain St George would find her—and just as frightened that he would. She didn't want to seem stammering and silly in his company, but she was sure she would. She seemed to quite forget everything else when she looked into his dark eyes.

'Miss Parker? Time for our dance, I think?' she heard his deep voice say behind her.

She spun around to face him and his easy smile made her feel instantly more at ease. 'Oh—of course. Thank you, Captain.'

As Rose took Captain St George's arm and walked with him across the crowded room, she felt something most distinctly— odd. Something she had never had an inkling of before. Parties and gowns and flirtations had never held much appeal for her, not compared to the pleasures of the piano or a good book by the fire. Parties were for her mother and sister, because watching their enjoyment made Rose happy, too. Mama and Lily had far less fun in their lives than they deserved.

Yet now, being with Captain St George, Rose found *she* could have fun as well. It was quite astonishing and rather delightful. They followed the lead couple into the steps of the lively dance, holding hands, their feet nearly touching as she skipped around him. They joined hands with two other couples, moving in an intricate star until they had to wait at the end of the line. It moved in a wonderful, bright blur, the greatest fun she had ever had in a dance!

'I'm sorry I'm not much of a dancer,' he said as he spun her around, making her laugh.

'I think you are quite grand at it,' she answered. 'But then I almost always have to practise with Lily and she does have a tendency to step on my toes rather more than I would like.'

'I'll try not to do that, then,' he answered, his smile widening. 'I don't have the chance to dance much, either.'

'I would think not, if you are always on the march. Do you have the chance to be in society a great deal?'

'Not a great deal, but for a time my regiment was posted for training near Bath, which I admit I rather enjoyed.'

'I have never been there,' Rose answered with a sigh. 'And only once or twice to London. A large town must be delightful!'

'It's not so terrible,' he answered, his eyes crinkling at the corners in a most enticing way as he looked at her. 'But family parties are always the best.'

'Yes,' Rose answered, a bit out of breath as she looked up at him. 'Indeed they are.' And this one was turning out to be the best she could ever remember. 'I do like evenings at home, though Lily says they are dull. A book and a fine fire, a song at the piano.'

'It sounds quite perfect, Miss Parker. Exactly what I would want one day. Some music in the winter evenings, a welcoming fire after a walk in the garden...'

'Exactly so,' Rose said. For just an instant she had an image in her mind, a picture of herself and the Captain walking down a path arm in arm, the doors of a manor house open behind them to spill out welcoming golden light. Something like what her family had when she was a child, before her father died and they found out it was all a deception, before she realised having her own family, her own secure home, was not to be. But with this man, she could imagine it all, even if it was only for a moment.

They took their turn once more in the set and Captain St George almost lifted her from her feet as they swirled around, making her laugh again. She actually felt delicate in his strong arms, like a lady in a novel, small and dainty next to her hero. They spun, breathless, and ended in a low bow and curtsy.

But the dance ended much too soon and she had to let go of his hand. They made their way to the edge of the crowd and Rose glimpsed her mother standing near the open tall windows with Emma Carrington and Charles St George. They were laughing and Rose had to smile to see her mother's enjoyment. It *was* all going rather well, better than she could have expected when they set out from their cottage that evening.

Then she saw the lady standing beside Charles St George, smiling languidly at the mirth of the others. She seemed so beautiful as to be of some other world, even in the elegance of the Barton Park drawing room. Tall and willowy, she looked as if she should be posing as Athena in a draped gown and golden helmet, serenely smiling, above it all.

In reality, she wore a fashionable gown of blush-coloured silk, her red-gold hair piled high atop her head and fastened with a bandeau of cameos. She slowly waved her painted silk fan, her gaze skimming over the party.

Next to Rose, Captain St George's tall figure stiffened. Surprised, she glanced up at him and saw that his smile had faded. The man she had danced with, so easy and kind, had vanished. He looked darkly intent. Full of a night-like desire.

'St George, there you are at last,' Athena called and something inside of Rose, something soft and summer-like that had bloomed so unexpectedly, faded. She felt suddenly cold inside and she wanted to turn and run, to disappear back into the crowd. Why had she thought even for a moment she could be something besides plain, sensible Rose Parker?

Captain St George stepped away, not completely, not really, but he definitely withdrew in some ineffable way. He was not quite there any longer.

The lady glided towards them and took the Captain's arm in her silk-gloved hand. They looked intently into each other's eyes and her smile widened. 'I am terribly sorry I'm late,' she said. 'I do hope you were not too bored. I know you do hate such parties.'

'I am not much for crowds, of course,' he answered. 'But Barton Park is different.'

'So I see.' Her gaze slid to Rose and her smile turned down at the edges. She glanced up and down Rose's made-over gown and glanced away, obviously finding her to be of not much interest.

'Miss Helen Layton, may I present a cousin of the Bancrofts?' Captain St George said. 'Miss Rose Parker. Miss Parker, this is an old friend of my family, Miss Layton.'

'An old friend, my dear St George?' Miss Layton said with a creamy laugh. 'Surely more than that. We have known each other since we were veritable babies. Charles says he expects an—well, an interesting announcement at any moment.'

An interesting announcement? Surely, Rose thought, that could only mean one thing. Captain St George and Miss Layton were a couple. She felt even colder, more foolish.

'It's a pleasure to meet you, Miss Layton,' she managed to say in a calm, steady voice.

'I think I just met your mother, Miss Parker,' Miss Layton said. She wafted her fan towards Rose's mother, who was still chatting with Emma and Charles St George. 'She says you live in a cottage nearby. How absolutely charming that sounds. Like Wordsworth, with roses round the door and sheep on the hills.'

Rose laughed, thinking of their smoking chimney and the vegetables she tried to grow in the kitchen garden mud, her chickens pecking around them. 'Something of the sort, I suppose, Miss Layton.'

'We must find something just the same when you get back from this silliness in Sicily,' Miss Layton said, her fingers curling around his sleeve.

He only gave her a tight smile and Rose could feel her cheeks turning warm as she longed even more to flee the whole uncomfortable scene.

'Rose! Rose!' she suddenly heard Lily cry and Rose had never been so relieved to see her sister. Rose spun around, away from the sight of the handsome Captain St George and the lovely Miss Layton, away from the foolish feelings that had come over her only moments ago.

Lily was running towards her, her face shining with happiness, utterly unconcerned with the impropriety of calling out and running at a ball. Mr Hewlitt followed her, just as glowing. Together they hurried towards Rose's mother, who was watching them avidly.

'Mrs Parker,' he said, trying so very hard

to be solemn that it almost made Rose laugh. 'May I have the privilege of speaking to you for a moment? I know such things are not usually done at a dance...'

'Please, just follow me,' Emma said. 'You can use the library. It will surely be quiet there for a moment.'

As they hurried away, Lily held out her hand to Rose to display a small pearl ring. 'Oh, Rose! Isn't it the loveliest?'

Rose smiled, but she was afraid she might also start crying as well. The happiness of that moment, of her sister's dreams coming true just as her own fledgling, girlish ideas were nipped in the bud, was almost over-whelming. But she did the only thing she knew how to do. She laughed and hugged her sister tight.

'The loveliest, Lily. I know you will be so very happy.'

Over her sister's shoulder as Lily hugged her back, Rose glimpsed Captain St George, withdrawing to a quiet corner with his brother and Miss Layton. He gave her a small smile and it was so sad, so full of commis-eration and understanding, that Rose nearly burst into tears. How perfect that one dance had been! Rose liked her life, her independence, but just for that moment she seemed to glimpse, far in the distance, the glimmer of something—more. A real home.

Miss Layton whispered something in the Captain's ear and the two of them turned away together, beautiful and perfect, leaving Rose in her ordinary world once more.

Oh, well, she thought, laughing at herself just a bit. Ordinary life was not so very bad after all.

'You will be a lovely bride, Lily dearest,' she said, squeezing her sister a little tighter before she let her go.

'And then it will be your turn, Rose, I vow it,' Lily said. 'I will find you someone just as handsome and sweet as my own Hewlitt.'

Rose closed her eyes, and saw, in the darkness of her mind, far away from the colour and noise of the party, Captain St George's all too brief smile. 'Oh, Lily. I don't think that would even be possible.'

The carriage was blessedly shadowed and silent as it jolted away from the lights of Barton Park and slid into the night. Harry leaned his head back against the leather cushions and closed his eyes, letting all the wondrous quiet wash over him.

Silence had become a precious commodity to him in the last few years. In Spain, and then at Waterloo, noise had been ever-present. The cacophony of military camps, drumbeats and shouted orders, and drunken laughter at night as men tried to forget their fears and loneliness around campfires. The explosion of shot and shell, the screams of people and horses as they fell, the sobbing afterward. No—quiet had no place in war.

Nor, it seemed, in a world after the war. Harry had returned to England thinking he was coming home to a world of green and rain and peace, the world he dreamed of in canvas tents at night. It had taken him years to return, but he had always been determined he would.

But it was not like that at all once he returned to London. There were parties all the time, dinners and teas and dances, with everyone clamouring for tales of the glorious heroics of war. He could hardly tell them the truth of it all, of the mud and blood and dying, so he said little at all. Charming social conversation had always been Charles's forte, not his.

Yet his silence only seemed to make him more sought out. Made more invitations arrive at his lodgings, more ladies want to sit beside him in drawing rooms or ride in the park. 'Like a corsair warrior in a poem,' he had once heard a lady whisper to her friend as they watched him at a musicale.

The memory made him laugh all over again. Him—a poetic corsair. If only they knew. He was just a rough army man, riding behind the drum, ever since he was a lad with his first commission. An army man with dreams of being a country farmer one day, of sitting by his own hearth after a day of watching his fields ripen and his sheep grow fat. A house where there was quiet all the time, except perhaps for a toddler's giggle or the sound of a lady playing at her pianoforte.

It was a dream that would have to be postponed again, at least for a time. His regiment had called on him once more, to go to sun-baked Sicily this time to put down a rebellion. There was only time for this one visit home, to his father's house at Hilltop Grange near Barton Park.

He hadn't wanted to go to the party at Barton. Yet more noise, more clamour, more stares. But Jane and Emma Bancroft were old neighbours, kind people, and he let Charles persuade him to attend. Now he was rather glad he had.

He closed his eyes and there he saw something most unexpected—the face of Miss Rose Parker. She had the sweetest smile he could remember ever seeing and even dancing, which he normally loathed, was a pleasure when he talked to her. She seemed almost like no lady, no person, he had ever met before. So calm, so serene—she made the very air seem to sigh with relief around her.

After so long in the rough world of war, he had almost given up ever glimpsing pure sweetness in anything again. Yet there it was, in Rose Parker's smile.

Until Helen appeared. Helen—one of his oldest friends, the daughter of his late mother's best friend, a lady of such beauty she was called in London The Incomparable. The lady everyone had always expected he would marry.

'How changeable you are tonight, Harry,' Charles said. 'Laughing, then scowling—one hardly knows what to expect next.'

Harry opened his eyes to study his brother, who lolled on the opposite seat. His golden hair gleamed in the moonlight from the open window, the perfect aquiline features that had always made him their late mother's copy, her darling, were outlined like a classical cameo. Charles was the perfect Apollo wherever he went to Harry's Hephaestus, always laughing and easy-tempered, making everyone around him feel easy as well. But now that the party was behind him, even Charles looked almost—sad, as he had rather often since Harry returned to England. Harry couldn't help but wonder what was plaguing his brother.

Perhaps it was because Charles had been left all those years to deal with Hilltop and their father while Harry was at war. And their father was not a kind man at the best of times.

The house that had been their mother's pride, the glowing name she had loved, had been tarnished by him.

'I laugh because the party went better than I could have expected,' he said.

'Ha!' Charles answered. 'So you see I was right to make you attend. The Bancroft girls are always kindness itself.'

'They are hardly girls now, are they? Jane a countess, Emma a widow.'

'Poor Emma. Remember when Mother made us go to the children's tea parties at Barton and we all ended up climbing trees instead?' Charles said with a laugh. 'Father was never happy at all when we came home with our best new coats torn and muddy. He said Mother was raising monkeys.'

'And the switches would come out.' The switches so often came out with their father, especially after their mother died. 'But it was always worth it to visit Barton Park.'

'Wasn't it, though? Like a different world.'

Harry nodded. *A different world.* He thought of Miss Parker's tales of searching for lost Royalist treasures there at Barton and wondered why they had never crossed paths as children. What would it have been like if they had?

'La belle Helen was in fine looks tonight,' Charles said. 'If only we had a thousand ships that needed to be launched…'

Harry frowned at the reminder of Helen and her elegant face flashed in his mind, erasing Miss Parker's gentle smile. The weight of expectation, the weight of what had been and what was expected in the future, fell once again. 'Helen has always been lovely.'

'Did Miss Lily Parker's sweet little engagement not inspire you, Harry? No ring for Helen's pretty finger yet?'

Harry wasn't sure he liked something in Charles's tone, something dark and hard beneath his smile. 'Helen knows this is no time for an engagement. I am to re-join my regiment soon and I would not tie her down to someone like myself.'

'You may think that, but does she? The betting books in the London clubs were full of speculation about when she would snap you into the parson's mousetrap. Everyone's expected it since we were children.'

Harry frowned as he stared out the window, at the summer moon shining on the silent hedgerows. 'You have picked up some ridiculous slang in those clubs of yours, Charlie.'

'Well, a man has to find distractions, you know. Hilltop Grange is not exactly a haven of merriment. And everyone says you and Helen were made for each other. Any man would give his right arm to be in your position.'

Something in his brother's voice caught Harry's strict attention, something sharp and jagged that was quite unlike Charles. He swung around to face him, but Charles's face was hidden in the shadows.

'Made for each other?' Harry said. Perhaps it was so—they had been friends for so long, bound by the long ties of their families, by their mothers' wishes. He had thought of her when he was gone, dreamed of her, carried her miniature with him to inspire him. She was like a dream, just as all that green English quiet had been a reason to come home.

And by Jove but she *was* beautiful. The most beautiful lady in London, just as all those silly, betting-book dandies declared.

For some reason, though, she seemed to prefer Harry to all those other men, at least for now.

But would Helen ever like that farm life he so envisioned? The quiet evenings, the small community? He was not at all sure. Perhaps that was what really held him back now.

Again he saw Miss Parker's sweet smile, felt her gentle touch on his hand, but he pushed such thoughts away.

'She agrees we should wait until I can resign my commission and we can see what happens next,' he said.

Charles shook his head, frowning. 'You should be careful, then, Harry. While you are gone on your adventures, someone else could easily pluck up such a prize. They do say that the Duke of Hamley, now that his time of mourning is at an end, seeks a new duchess.'

Harry laughed. Duchess—now there was a role that would suit Helen well. 'No one would make a better duchess than Helen.'

Charles was silent for a long, tense moment. 'I would never have taken you for a fool, Harry.'

Before Harry could answer, their carriage

turned through the gates of Hilltop Grange and jolted up the winding old drive, past the overgrown forest that had once been a manicured garden under the careful eye of their mother.

Now, Hilltop looked nothing like the golden welcome of Barton Park, which had seemed to float above the night like a cloud of light. Hilltop had no light at all, save the glow of one lamp in the window of the library. Harry knew that once daylight came, the overgrown ivy on the grey stone walls, the crumbling chimneys, the covered windows, would all be too apparent. He felt again that deep pang of sadness, of guilt for following a different duty.

But that one light meant their father was still awake, or more likely fallen asleep next to his empty brandy bottle. He seldom left the library now.

'Our great inheritance,' Charles said, his tone quiet and bitter.

Harry gave a grim nod. 'I am sorry, Charles. I should have been here all along.'

Charles glanced at him, his expression startled. 'Oh, no, Harry, never. You are doing what you have to—your duty to King and Country as you are called to do. No one has been more dutiful than you, ever since we were children.'

He thought again of what their home had once been, what it was now. 'I don't know about that.'

'Well, I do. Whatever I face here with Father is as nothing compared to whatever you have faced all these years. Besides, I'm seldom here at Hilltop at all these days.' He grinned and that strange, solemn, thoughtful Charles vanished. The rakish, fun-loving young man everyone knew was back. 'London is much more diverting. Why would a man ever live anywhere else?'

'Diverting—and expensive,' Harry muttered, but he couldn't help laughing at Charles's devil-may-care smile. It was always thus with his younger brother, their mother's golden boy. While Charles was the fun one, Harry had indeed always been the responsible one. The quiet one.

Charles shrugged. 'What else can one do? I would be wretched in the army, worse than useless. The church would never have me.'

'What of your painting?' he asked, remembering the rare talent Charles once possessed with a brush, the way he could capture the mood of a landscape in a few deft strokes of paint.

Charles laughed. 'A boy's diversion. Not fit for a grown man, y'know.'

'According to who? Our father?' Harry asked quietly.

Rather than answer, Charles pushed open the carriage door as soon as they came to a full halt and jumped down. Harry followed him up the shallow stone steps into the echoing hall of Hilltop Grange. In the shadows, the portraits of their ancestors, including their golden-haired mother, watched them in silence. In the rooms beyond, the furniture was shrouded in canvas covers, like ghosts. Their mother's cherished pianoforte was silent.

For just an instant, Harry had such a different vision of the house, light gleaming on polished wood. The warmth of the fire, the scent of flowers from the gardens, the rush of small feet down the stairs, music. But the lady who turned from the keyboard to welcome him with a smile—her eyes were the sweet, soft hazel of Rose Parker.

'Father, wake up!' Charles shouted, banging on the library door with his fist. The dream was shattered, like the dust of Hilltop itself.

Chapter One

‹‹‹‹‹‹‹~~~~~›››››››

Winter, three years later

'Jouissons dans nos asiles, jouissons de biens tranquilles! Ah, peut-on être heureux, quand on forme d'autres vouex?'

'That's quite enough!' Aunt Sylvia shouted from her armchair near the fire, where she was swathed in shawls and a fur blanket. Her three lapdogs shifted and barked. 'What a wretched song by that horrid Rameau. Why would you play such a thing?'

Rose sighed and rested her wrists on the edge of the keyboard as the last notes died away in the overheated drawing room of Aunt Sylvia's vast house. She would have laughed if she wasn't quite so tired. She removed her spectacles and rubbed at her eyes. In her years of working as Aunt Sylvia's companion, she had come to learn no moment was predictable. A favourite food one day, which had to be ordered from London and fetched from the village shop, a two-mile walk, by Rose every day, would not be wanted once it arrived. An expensive pelisse would be dismissed as too itchy, then needed again. The wheeled Bath chair would have to be fetched for a walk in the garden, only to be greeted with shouts of 'What do you think I am, an old invalid? I shall walk! Give me your arm immediately, Rose. You cannot be rid of me so easily, you know, you silly girl.'

Rose did not want to be rid of Aunt Sylvia. She paid a wage that kept Rose's mother in her cottage, now that Lily and Mr Hewlitt had two children to take care of in their small vicarage and Mama's small income seemed even smaller than ever. Her mother deserved to stay in her own home and Rose had to work to make it so. But Rose *did* wish Aunt Sylvia would make up her mind for once.

'I thought you always enjoyed the old

French songs, Aunt,' she said. 'Because they reminded you of your time at Versailles.'

In her youth, Aunt Sylvia had once waited upon Queen Marie Antoinette, before she married the wealthy Mr Pemberton and returned to England. She spoke of it all the time and definitely never let anyone forget it, with her grey hair piled high and panniers strangely paired with newer, higher waists and puffed sleeves.

'Why would I want to hear songs that remind me of such a terrible loss?' Aunt Sylvia said, thumping her walking stick on the floor. One of the dogs barked. 'You young people, you know nothing of such things. Nothing of how fortunate you all are.'

Rose suddenly remembered Captain St George and their dance at the midsummer party so long ago, the haunted look in his dark eyes as he mentioned battle and seemed to remember Waterloo. She had thought of him too often in the years since, especially in the long, quiet nights as she lay awake waiting for Aunt Sylvia to call her. Had he married the beautiful Miss Layton, had he come back from battle and found peace at last? She couldn't help but hope so.

She glanced out the window, out the slim rectangle of thick glass revealed between the heavy brocade curtains Aunt Sylvia kept closed all the time. It had started snowing, a light, lacy, delicate pattern of white against the night sky. It reminded her that it was nearly December, nearly the Christmas season, and she wondered what her mother, what Lily and her little family, were doing now.

Lily and her babies were surely decorating their small sitting room with greenery, baking plum cakes to carry to Mr Hewlitt's parishioners. Perhaps her mother was embroidering new little gowns to wrap up for her grandchildren's gifts.

She felt the familiar pang of sadness of missing them and she had to remind herself why she had to work in the first place.

'Perhaps I could play you a Christmas carol or two, Aunt Sylvia?' she said. 'It is nearly that season.'

'Christmas!' Aunt Sylvia cried. 'Don't even talk to me about the wretched thing.

Play some Mozart. You know how I always like that.'

Except for when she called Mozart an overrated performing monkey of a boy. Rose smothered a laugh, and launched into the 'Allegro' from *Marriage of Figaro*. Just as she always could, she soon lost herself in the music, and the harsh world of Aunt Sylvia's house, her loneliness for her family, vanished. She floated in her own realm, above everything else.

One day, she thought with a happy smile, perhaps she would have her own home with her own pianoforte. Could play whatever she chose, while her family listened...

The piece ended and Rose felt as if she was pushed out of that magical, floating world into the stuffy drawing room. Suddenly all she could hear were the snores of her aunt, mixed with the softer snuffles of the dogs and the crackle of the flames as a log collapsed into ashes in the grate. She remembered how her childhood home had once collapsed, how such things were always dreams.

She peeked over her shoulder to find Aunt Sylvia had indeed fallen asleep, her head lolling back on her cushioned chair. Hardly daring to breathe, for fear she would awaken everyone and prolong the evening, Rose carefully lowered the lid of the pianoforte over the keys and slid off the stool. She cautiously tiptoed over to make sure Aunt Sylvia's shawls were still warmly tucked around her, and then crept out of the drawing room. She found Miss Powell, her aunt's long-suffering maid, waiting outside.

Rose gave her a nod, which Miss Powell tersely returned, and at last Rose could make her way up the stairs to her own chamber. It was not a large room at all, barely big enough for a narrow bed, a washstand and her trunk, and it looked down on the frost-covered kitchen gardens, but it was at least her own. In the cottage at home, she had shared with Lily until they could build on an extra room and her sister's feet at night were always freezing.

And then she missed her sister and mother all over again.

'Don't be such a goose,' she told herself sternly. Surely it was only the Christmas season making her feel so melancholy now, so homesick. She had too much to do to worry about Mama and Lily now. Aunt Sylvia would want her up early as usual, writing letters and walking the dogs.

As she dug around in her clothes trunk for her night chemise, hoping her sheets wouldn't be too chilled by the time she crawled between them, there was a knock at the door. Surprised anyone would be about at that hour—Aunt Sylvia dined early and only Miss Powell stayed up to help her retire—she hurried to answer it.

One of the young housemaids stood there, yawning into her apron. 'Beg your pardon, miss, but these came for you by the afternoon post, but I forgot to give them to you. We do get that busy with the tea things…'

Rose shuddered to remember the row with Aunt Sylvia and the undercooked almond cakes that afternoon. 'That is quite all right, thank you.' She took the letters eagerly as the maid hurried away.

One from Lily, she saw, recognising her sister's hurried scrawl. And one with a grander seal, pressed into fashionable green wax. *Barton Park*, the return address read.

A letter from Barton! Rose felt the warm touch of excitement, and not a little tinge of curiosity. She hadn't heard from Barton Park in quite some time. She knew Jane had been busy with having little heirs to the earldom, and Emma had recently married David Marton, one of their neighbours.

Rose quickly changed into her nightdress, carefully laying aside her sensible grey-silk gown, and climbed into bed to read the precious missives. She opened the one from Barton first. It was written in elegant dark green ink on thick, creamy stationery.

My dear Miss Parker—or may I call you Cousin Rose?

I am so sorry we have not met since Cousin Lily's wedding. We do miss your family so much and speak often of how your letters make us laugh. Your tales of being with Aunt Sylvia—dear lady, but, well, she is Aunt Sylvia after all—are better than a comic novel and cheer us to no end. You are a brave lady indeed.

We also speak often of that lovely midsummer ball when Lily and her vicar became engaged. It seems so very long since Barton has enjoyed such an evening.

Hayden has duties in the House of Lords which often take him to London, and as you know we now have four dear children—William, Eleanor, Emma and baby Edward.

Emma and David are also expecting a happy occasion soon and Emma still has her little bookshop in the village. She does insist on scrambling up and down the library ladders, frightening her husband no end, but she declares she has never felt better in her life!

I do envy her. My own times bring nothing but sleepiness. I often nod off by the fire quite like Aunt Sylvia!

Rose smiled at the image of Jane, nodding off by the fire as her children dashed about. She pushed away the hint of envy such an image gave her and continued reading.

In short, dear Cousin Rose, I have a great favour to ask. Emma and I have decided to revive our old Barton parties, this time for the Christmas holidays. It has indeed been a long time since we had such festivities here and the children would so enjoy it.

Their governess, though, wishes to return to her family for a few weeks and I am quite overwhelmed. If Aunt Sylvia could spare you, and if you think you could bear us and our noise, would a position here suit you for a time?

I remember how you loved music and my own little Eleanor shows great talent at the pianoforte and harp already. Aunt Sylvia is, of course, invited as well, if she can ever leave her own hearth. Fingers crossed that she is quite comfortable in situ, though!

I do hope so, dear Rose, as we would dearly love to see you again and have your assistance with our little monsters. If you like us, perhaps a longer stay here at Barton might be possible?

With much hope,

Your cousin, Jane Ramsay

Rose lowered the letter with a thoughtful frown. She well remembered when they discovered the disaster of her late father's debts, the wreck of her mother's annuity and the near loss of their cottage. Jane had been all that was kind at the time, offering assistance of every sort from financial gifts to a new home at Barton. Yet Rose and her mother had been so loathe to take charity, even from family. The position with Aunt Sylvia was just that—a position, with wages for tasks and long hours. Not perfect, not merry or fun, but it got them by and let her mother stay in her home.

She wondered if Jane's offer now was also charity, carefully disguised as a temporary governess–music teacher position, but she found she didn't quite care. She closed her eyes and remembered Barton Park, how pretty it was, how welcoming, how full of fun. She remembered her dance there with Captain St George, the bright, hopeful way he had made her feel. Maybe she would find a spark of that again, there at Barton at Christmas?

She tucked the letter under her pillow, along with Lily's to save for a morning treat, and blew out her candle. She closed her eyes again and hoped to dream of music and mistletoe and dances with handsome partners…

'Jane, surely it is nearly midnight. Put that away and come to bed,' Hayden Fitzwalter, Earl of Ramsay, said, patting at the feather pillows next to him on their large, luxurious feather mattress.

Jane laughed, but she didn't look up from the pile of papers on her writing desk. She knew if she saw her gorgeous husband, his dark hair tousled, half-naked in their lovely warm bed, she would never finish her work at all. Even after years of marriage, those gorgeous blue eyes of his were too tempting indeed.

'I only have a few more invitations to write and they must go out with the morning post,' she said, her pen scratching over her creamy paper. 'We are going to have the grandest Christmas house party Barton Park has ever seen! We will have carols and wassail, and sleigh rides…'

Hayden laughed. 'Sleigh rides? What if there is no snow, my love?'

'Then we shall make some. It's the first Christmas we've all been together at Barton in ages.' They spent most of their time now in London, or at Hayden's earldom seat. But Barton, where her own parents had once been so happy and raised Emma and herself in a golden childhood, was always home. 'When Emma and I were children, our parents made the holidays so magical. Such games and music, and wonderful sweets on the tables. Green wreaths and dancing. I want it to be just like that now for the children.'

'And so it shall be, if *you* will it so. Everything you create in our lives is magic, my love.'

She looked over at him and smiled. 'Our lives *are* magical—now. If I can help someone else find the same thing…'

'Ah, I see.' His tone was full of smug satisfaction and he crossed his arms behind his head as he laid back on the pillows. 'Trying a bit of matchmaking, are you? Who do you and Emma have in mind now?'

Jane pursed her lips. 'No one at all, of course. If people just happen to meet at our party and just happen to like each other—

well, how can that be a bad thing? Magical things *do* happen at Christmas.'

'So they do. Who are you inviting, then?'

Jane glanced over her list and named a few of their London friends she thought might enjoy Barton. Her old family house was small compared to Hayden's grand seat and there was not space for very many. There was definitely no space for Hayden's old rakish friends, from the dark days before they mended their marriage and started their family.

'Also, Mr and Mrs Hewlitt, though I'm not sure he can be spared from his clerical duties for the holiday,' she said.

'That is too bad. I remember when they became betrothed at Barton.'

'I know, wasn't it terribly sweet?' Jane said. 'I also asked her sister, Miss Rose Parker. I'm sure you remember her, too.'

'Of course. A most sensible and cheerful lady. Her performance of Beethoven at the pianoforte was impressive.'

'I hope she is still sensible and cheerful. She has been working as companion to Sylvia Pemberton.'

'Oh, that poor girl!' Hayden exclaimed. 'Will the kraken release its captive to come to Barton?'

'I am afraid I performed a bit of a subterfuge, since I know how proud Rose is and how their family has been brought so low of late. I told her we would need a governess for the children while Miss Essex is gone for the holidays and that Eleanor shows a proficiency for music, which she does.'

'Jane! You've just moved her from working for one monster to four.'

Jane laughed. 'Hayden! They are very well-behaved children, everyone says so.'

'Well behaved in public, maybe,' Hayden muttered, but Jane could hear the affectionate pride in his voice.

'The nursemaids will all still be here. I did have to lure Rose here somehow, or she wouldn't leave Aunt Sylvia and would have a miserable Christmas.' And there would be no chances for her to meet eligible young men if she didn't come to the party.

'Quite right. Who else have you invited, then?'

Jane hesitated as she looked down at the

last invitation on her desk. 'The St George brothers, at Hilltop.'

'Is that quite wise? Harry has not been home long, and he has not received any visitors yet. He might not be quite—recovered.'

'When Dr Heath called last week, he told me he found Captain St George's health to be much improved last time he was at Hilltop, though not entirely as he once was, of course. A Christmas party might be just the chance to cheer him up! After all he has been through—being wounded and losing Miss Layton…'

'You mean Lady Fallon?' Hayden said quietly.

'The Dowager Lady Fallon now, not that it matters,' Jane answered. That sudden marriage, after Captain St George left for Sicily, had surprised everyone. But if Jane had learned one thing in life, it was that everyone had secrets they hid deep down inside. Everyone deserved a second chance. 'If the Captain does not yet feel like a party, he can always refuse. But I am inviting him, as well as his brother, Charles, who I hear is back from the Continent now.' And Charles had always been such fun; maybe Rose Parker could use a bit of that fun in her life.

'You must do what you think best, my love. Yet now it really *is* time to come to bed. It grows much too late.'

'And much too cold, with you so far over there,' she said with a laugh, thinking how lucky they were indeed to have had their own second chance. Their life together.

She sealed up the last invitation, the one bound for Hilltop Grange, and snuffed out the candles before she hurried into the warm haven of her husband's loving arms.

Chapter Two

'Aye, 'tis a pity. Hilltop Grange was once so grand. Now look at it. Falling to bits.'

'Some who has it all haven't the sense to appreciate it. Fritter it all away. Shameful.'

'Oh, you two,' the barmaid tsked to the two old men as she plopped fresh pints down on their sticky, scarred table. 'Always grumbling 'bout something and not doing a thing about it. Now that the Captain is back…'

'Will he be any better than that brother of his? Or the father?' one old man muttered. 'Been gone for years, ain't he?'

'He has to care, doesn't he? Hilltop is his estate now,' the barmaid said as she turned away, wiping her hands on her apron. The two old men returned to the weather, to the threat of snow in the air.

None of them seemed to notice Harry sitting quietly in the darkest corner of the pub, the new owner of Hilltop Grange, nursing his ale and pondering what he had to do next.

He took a long drink from his tankard, but even that did not warm him. A few snowflakes drifted past the grimy windows, landing lightly on the cobbled streets of the village outside. A few people hurried past, stepping out of the greenery-bedecked shops, their arms laden with Christmas packages, laughing together in holiday cheer, brushing the snow off their cloaks and hats.

It wasn't the grey winter sky that made him feel so cold, or the joy in the coming holiday that he saw in others but barely remembered ever having himself. It was a numbness at his very core that had probably always been there, ever since Waterloo, when he realised the true ugliness of life.

No, he thought in sudden, startled remembrance. It hadn't *always* been thus. For one moment, long ago, it had lifted, like a tiny spark of sun through those clouds. When he held a hazel-eyed girl in his arms for a dance, and she laughed with him, those eyes shining with her enjoyment of the music and of all the life around them. He knew just for a small instant, with her, the sweetness he was really fighting for.

Miss Rose Parker. That was her name. And she'd looked like a rose, too, with the faint pink in her pale cheeks. Surely she was Mrs Rose Some-Other-Surname now, with a baby in her arms. Whoever he was—well, he was a lucky bloke indeed. Harry just hoped he appreciated what he had.

He touched the black patch over his lost eye, feeling the roughness of the skin around it, the scar that curved its way almost to his jaw. What would Rose Parker think if she saw him now? Would her smiles turn to startled fear, to quickly averted glances just like everyone else? Just like it had with Helen?

Harry gave a humourless little laugh. No, not Helen. She'd left long before the wounds; she'd left when someone with more to offer, with a title even, came around. Not that Harry could blame her, not a bit. Being a soldier's wife would never have suited Helen, no matter how much she once protested otherwise, how much their families wished otherwise. And now with Hilltop in the state it was...

Harry finished his tankard and pushed back his chair. Speaking of Hilltop, he knew he should be getting back there. He had lingered in the village too long after his visit to the lawyer Mr Wall. Hilltop would never have its roof and windows fixed by sitting around in taverns. The problem was—he wasn't sure yet how to fix it all. He knew the army, that was all. Now he had to learn how to be a landlord to a crumbled estate.

The barmaid appeared at his side. She looked at him with a twinge of pity in her eyes, but she didn't turn away.

'Another pint, then, Captain?' she said. 'Or maybe some wine? We just got some bottles, special for the season.'

He gave her a smile. 'Not today, Nell, but next time. And it's just Mr now, not Captain.'

He left the tavern, striding past the grumbling old men without a word and out into the world. For an instant, his eye was dazzled by the bright grey glare of the light after the dim tavern. He pulled the brim of his hat lower and raised the collar of his greatcoat against the cold breeze. He was still trying to become accustomed to the way having sight in only one eye distorted the horizon.

The village was not a large one, but it was very busy at that time of day, as shoppers finished their last-minute errands before hurrying home to their warm fires. He knew every shop from when he was a child—the butcher, where Christmas geese and hams now waited in his window, the dressmaker, where his mother had had so many gowns sewn up, the confectioner, from whom he and Charles used to steal lemon drops.

All the doors were wreathed in greenery now, all the window displays decked in bows. The Christmas atmosphere of his home village was so very familiar, but so very alien at the same time. A dream world.

Harry turned towards the livery stable where he had left his horse. On the corner, an old man was selling bouquets of mistletoe and holly tied with red ribbon, and Harry impulsively bought one. He wasn't sure what he would do with it, but for a moment the red brightened his thoughts.

He passed by the bookshop that had once

been owned by old Mr Lorne, but which he had heard now belonged to Emma Bancroft, or Lady Marton as she had become. He paused to examine the display in her bow window, the leather-bound volumes with their gilded lettering gleaming, the boxes of fine stationery. He remembered his mother going there every month for her new stock of novels from London.

The shop door swung open with a jangle of bells, and Emma Marton hurried out, nearly bumping into him. The young girl behind her, who must be her stepdaughter, the young Beatrice Marton, caught her as she stumbled and laughed. Emma looked as if she had not aged at all while he'd been gone, her blond curls still as sunny, her smile still dimpled. Like the village, she seemed to have stayed still while he felt centuries older.

But not everything had stayed the same. Under the folds of her green-velvet cloak, he could see the small bump of a child, one of the growing brood of Bancroft Park.

He remembered how once Barton had seemed as crumbling and lonely as Hilltop, and the Bancroft sisters had raised it back life. It gave him a spark of hope now to think of it.

'Oh, Harry!' Emma cried, her gaze flickering over his scarred face and then quickly away. 'How perfectly wonderful to see you home. We all so feared for your health when—well, when we heard what happened and...well—' Her words broke off and she blushed under the brim of her feathered bonnet.

He smiled down at her. 'I left one or two bits behind on the battlefield, but am now in good health, thank you, Emma. As I see are you. You are quite blooming.'

She laughed, turning even pinker. 'Oh, yes! In a few months, Bea here will be a sister again. You do remember Miss Beatrice Marton, my stepdaughter?'

The girl dropped a shy little curtsy as Harry bowed. She was a pretty thing, with dark hair smooth under her hood and sweet eyes; one day she would surely break hearts. 'Of course. How do you do, Miss Marton?'

'I am quite well, thank you, Captain St George.'

'I couldn't do without Bea's help at home

and here at the shop,' Emma said proudly, taking Beatrice's hand. 'Especially now that Christmas is so near. I do hope we will see you at Barton.'

'I'm afraid there is still much to do at Hill-top,' he answered. Christmas was for family and good cheer, not for staring at wounded soldiers. He did not want to be the ghost at the feast.

'Oh, but you must,' Beatrice said warmly. 'There can surely be nothing merrier than the holiday Aunt Jane has planned. Games and sleigh rides and plum pudding...'

'Oh, Bea, I'm sure Captain St George knows how he wants to spend his holiday,' Emma said, squeezing her stepdaughter's hand. 'But do know you are always most welcome at our homes, Harry, any time at all.'

'Thank you, Emma. That does mean much to me.' He impulsively handed her the bouquet of greenery he had bought. 'Happy Christmas.'

He turned and walked away, but when he glanced back Emma was watching him with a thoughtful frown. She quickly smiled and waved the bouquet, the red ribbon a banner of brightness against the grey day.

Unlike the village, Hilltop did not bustle with holiday preparations and cheer. The windows were blank in the gathering twilight as Harry rode up the overgrown lane; no smoke curled from the crumbling chimneys. There were, however, a few more fallen roof slates on the portico and in the tangled flowerbeds.

As Harry swung down from the saddle, he studied the house and for just an instant he remembered what it had been like in his mother's day, with the flowers blooming and bright against the pale grey walls, curtains elegant in every window. He could imagine a lady like Rose Parker in such a house, but not this one.

Then he blinked and the fantasy of a smiling lady welcoming him home was replaced with reality once more.

He left his horse with the young stable lad, one of the few servants left at Hilltop along with their ancient butler Jenkins, and hurried up the front steps into the darkening house.

The doors to the drawing room and music room were firmly shut, the few pieces of furniture in the hall shrouded in dust cloths. Yet it was not quite as silent as he expected. The door to the library was half-open, and a bar of amber-gold spilled out. He heard the clink of heavy crystal, as if a decanter had just been plonked down on a table.

Curious, and not a little irritated that someone would break into his solitude uninvited, Harry tossed his hat and gloves on to the nearest canvas-covered table and strode towards the library.

The room was just as he had left it, half-empty and dusty, most of the books sold or packed away, but his brother, Charles, sat behind their father's desk. His dark gold hair was over-long and mussed, his buff travel coat dusty and a half-empty brandy bottle sat before him.

He looked up and Harry saw that his blue eyes were rimmed with red. He remembered the last time he'd seen Charles, when his brother was leaving for the Continent. To paint, he said, but more likely to get away from their father. 'My brother! The returning hero,' Charles called, raising his almost empty glass. 'Let me pour you a drink. You probably need it after meeting with old Mr Wall. That's where Jenkins said you were, anyway.'

Harry sat down across from him, stretching his long legs before him. He had learned long ago not to wonder about Charles's comings and goings. 'I've just come from the tavern and it looks as if you've already started the celebrating.'

Charles examined his glass. 'So I have. 'Tis the merry season, after all.'

'So everyone keeps telling me. Where have you been lately, Charlie?'

'Oh, here and there. Italy mostly. Then some German spa towns. Until I heard you were home.'

'Not doing your art, then?' Harry asked. Charles had always been a masterful artist, one who could be a professional in Harry's uneducated opinion, though their father had scoffed at it all.

Charles frowned. 'No, not really. Too busy with other matters.'

Harry nodded, but he said nothing. He

didn't really want to know what those 'other matters' were.

Charles poured them each another measure. 'What did Wall say?'

Harry took a deep drink of the brandy. It was the last of their father's stock and not bad at all as it burned down his throat. 'About what you would expect he would say. Mother's money was spent long ago and there are debts on the estate.'

Charles sighed. 'I think there is only one solution, then, my dear brother.'

Harry laughed. 'Sell Hilltop and go back in the army? They don't want a one-eyed captain. Maybe you could get a job in the City?'

Charles shuddered. 'Lud, no. How appalling. I could never have a job, and I certainly don't want my brother nearly killed again.'

'I'm glad you care.' Harry thought of how it was when they were children, running together through the fields, jumping into the pond. And how far apart they were now.

''Course I do. You're the only brother I have. And I don't think we *can* sell Hilltop.'

'Indeed not. Even if it weren't entailed in the St George family, no one would want it.'

'Exactly. Ghastly old pile.'

'Then what is your solution?'

'Very simple. You must marry an heiress,' Charles said.

Harry laughed even harder. 'You always did have a fine way with a joke, Charlie.'

Charles scowled. 'I am absolutely serious. A lady, one with style and a fine dowry, would fix things in a trice.'

Harry shook his head. Even before he was wounded, his wooing skills had not been the greatest. To think of trying to win a fair, rich lady now—he laughed again. 'Who would you suggest, then? Has a blind heiress come on to the market, perhaps? One who could tolerate a scarred old soldier?'

'You've always been far more handsome than you would admit, Harry. And now you're a wounded warrior. Ladies love that.' Charles paused to stare down into his glass. 'Helen Layton is recently widowed, you know. They say her husband left her well set-up indeed.'

Harry's smile faded and he swallowed the last of his drink. 'You know that was over long ago. I think *you* are the one who will have to find an heiress, Charlie. You always enjoyed society much more than me, anyway. You could take up painting again. Or you could go back to the Continent to look among the spas and casinos.'

'I doubt we would have to go so far. This came while you were out.' Charles slapped a letter down on the desk.

Harry gave it a suspicious glance. 'What is it? Another dunning letter?'

'Of course not. It's an invitation to a Christmas house party at Barton Park. Jane says there will be several ladies there, old friends and new.'

'Ah,' Harry muttered, pushing aside his glass. *Games and sleigh rides and plum pudding.* 'So that's what she meant.'

'She?'

'I saw Emma Marton in the village, she said something about Barton for the holiday. Thought it might be a good distraction.' And it might, he thought through the slight haze of the brandy as he studied the crumbling plaster of the ceiling. Anything would be better than looking at this room any longer.

'Well, I suppose somehow, some way, we have to try and save Hilltop,' Charles said.

'I know I've always been a useless wastrel, but…'

'No,' Harry said decisively. 'I am the eldest and this is indeed our family's home. We do have to save it and everyone who depends on it along with it. I will find a way.' *No matter what.*

Chapter Three

We are having a true, merry, family sort of holiday here at Barton Park, where we hope to see all our old friends.

We have not seen you seen you since Lord Fitzwalter attended Lord Fallon's funeral and we hope that your mourning will not deprive us of your company.

H*er mourning.* Helen, Dowager Lady Fallon, laughed as she dropped Jane Ramsay's letter at the side of the bathtub. She sank deeper into the rose-scented water and stared up at the painted tile ceiling of her bathing room in her London town house. Everyone had thought it so extravagant when she'd had it built on to her dressing room, with its marble walls and painted fireplace. But it was her favourite place, a small, cosy space where no one would bother her.

She had once thought being Lady Fallon would be a grand thing indeed, a life of ease and grandeur, full of pretty gowns and parties and fun. So different from her own family, their façade of liveliness and prosperity that hid a distinct lack of funds. She had given up Harry St George, so handsome and gallant, to marry a man thirty years older in order to get that life. But being Lady Fallon had not been what she'd expected.

It hadn't been worth it.

Helen sat up in the tub, the water frothing around her, and caught a glimpse of herself in her gilt-framed mirror. Her golden hair, curling with the damp air, her pink and white skin, it was all still youthful and beautiful. And she did have old Lord Fallon's money now, too. Surely it was not too late for her?

She reached for the letter again. *Old friends.* Did that mean Harry St George would be there? She had heard he had returned to England, more heroic than ever.

What could she not do in society, with her new money and a war hero at her side?

Maybe a Christmas in the country was just what she needed.

Charles St George swirled the brandy in his glass and stared out into the darkness of the night. Winter clouds had lowered, extinguishing the stars and moonlight, but that was good. In the darkness, the shambles of the garden at Hilltop, the garden their mother had once so loved, that he had painted so many times, could not be seen. It was just a blank, like everything else.

It was quiet, a lot like the way he felt inside, Charles thought as he took another drink. As if he watched the world from a great distance, not caring particularly what happened one way or another.

That was the real reason why he had drifted around the Continent for so long. Their father had so often declared him useless, why not be so? Harry had escaped it all in the army. Charles had once tried to escape in art, which he loved but could not ultimately find fulfilling, and then in spa towns.

But now, back here at Hilltop with his brother again, he found he *did* care. And it ate at him. Harry had given so much; he deserved more than a wastrel brother and a falling-down house that had once been loved. He just wished to heaven he knew what to do.

Perhaps Christmas at Barton Park would be a good thing. A bit of merriment amongst other people, other families, away from the constant blankness.

'Fa-la-la-la-la…' he muttered and finished off his brandy.

Chapter Four

'Barton Park is just ahead, miss. Nearly there now,' the coachman called out as they slowed at the crest of a hill.

Rose leaned out the window, eager for a glimpse of the house of which she had such happy memories. It hadn't been an unpleasant journey, with a valise full of books to read and no Aunt Sylvia shouting out demands, but it *had* been a cold one. The winter wind did like to nip through her mended gloves and snatch at her cloak. Surely there would be a good fire waiting at Barton.

But she found she was a bit nervous as well. It had been years since she saw her cousins last—what were they like now? What would they think of her?

They passed through an open iron gate, beautifully wrought and crowned with a gilded B. The drive was a long, winding one, designed at the height of the craze for picturesque landscapes under Jane and Emma's scholarly father, and Rose was enchanted by the view. Even in winter, with all the trees bare and frost thick on the ground, it was lovely.

As the coach meandered past groves of trees and hedges, she glimpsed pale marble statues, like ghosts in the grey day. In the distance, she saw the *chinoiserie* peaks of an old summerhouse and the stone walls that marked off Rose Hill, Emma's husband's estate next door. She remembered playing on those grounds as child, looking for treasure in the medieval ruins of the cold castle.

Suddenly there was a fork in the lane and they turned off to find the house itself.

It was not a large house, but it was a romantic one, warm and welcoming with its time-mellowed red-brick walls, its grey stone front steps and inlaid stone patterns around the windows. Smoke curled from the chimney in fragrant, silvery plumes. The doors were decorated with green wreaths tied with golden bows and evergreen plants lined the portico in silver-stained pots.

Much to Rose's surprise, as the coach rolled to a stop the front doors opened and a veritable herd of children tumbled out. The two tallest were obviously the twins, William and Eleanor, and they led two smaller children, probably Emma and Edward, and Eleanor held a toddler by the hand whose golden curls looked like those of her mother, Emma Marton. They were bundled against the cold in a bright, jewel-like cluster of green- and blue-velvet coats and cloaks.

The coachman lowered the steps and helped Rose to alight, and as soon as her boots touched the gravel the children launched into song.

"'Good King Wenceslaus looked out, on the feast of Stephen! When the snow lay round about, deep and crisp and even...'"

Rose couldn't help but laugh in delight at the sweet sound of their voices, carried by the cold, clear air. It seemed to encourage them to sing even louder, until they reached the end on a long, carrying note.

"'...gath'ring winter fu-u-uel!'"

'Welcome to Barton,' the tallest girl said. She stepped forward with a little curtsy, presenting Rose with a mistletoe bouquet.

Rose curtsied back, charmed by the song— and, she admitted, a little relieved, after the stories some of her friends who were governesses told about wild children ransacking workboxes and setting loose mice.

'That was most beautifully sung,' she said. 'I am sure not even one of the royal princesses could expect a finer welcome.'

'Oh, we've been practising for days and days!' the oldest boy said. 'We have a different song for every guest. You're the first one to arrive. Would you like to hear another? Mother said you're very good at music.'

Jane appeared in the doorway and laid a gentle hand on her son's shoulder. She did not look like a grand countess, Rose thought, with her hair pinned up in loose curls and a soft Indian shawl wrapped over her muslin day dress. She looked like the cousin she always remembered. 'William, dearest, I am sure Miss Parker is weary from her journey and wants to come in from the cold.'

'Oh, of course!' young William cried and the children surrounded her to sweep her into the hall. It had the same air of elegant informality as the outside of the house, with its black and white tiled floor softened by bright rugs. The balustrade of the staircase that swept up to the next story seemed bright and newly gilded, lined with a blue and gold carpet runner, the blue silk-striped walls were lined with blue satin chairs tossed with red cushions. A marble-topped table held a large bouquet of holly and ivy, which cast their fresh, green scent into the warm air.

Jane kissed Rose's cheeks, clasping her hands in welcome. 'Rose, my dear, I cannot tell you how happy I am to see you again! And how grateful for your help. With a houseful of guests on the way, I would not know how to manage with this pack of ruffians.'

Rose untied and removed her grey bonnet, studying the smiling, rosy-cheeked children around them. 'They look civilised enough to me.'

Jane laughed. 'That's only because they are on their best party behaviour at the moment. These are my eldest, the twins, William and Eleanor, who is quite the budding musician,' she said, as the children made their bows. 'And little Emma and my baby Edward, who is not such a baby now. The littlest is Emma's girl Martha. Emma has gone into the village with Beatrice, her lovely stepdaughter, to see about her bookshop, but will be here for dinner with her husband later.'

Rose smiled as she watched them, remembering their song and their promise of more. 'William said guests will be arriving soon?'

'Oh, yes, most of them by teatime, I hope. You are the first,' Jane said. She reached out and straightened the vase of greenery. 'So you will have plenty of time to rest before the merriment begins in earnest! I told Hannah, our old housekeeper, whom I am sure you remember, to make sure you have a good fire and some tea in your room. Perhaps a warm bath? I do hope the journey was not too chilling.'

Rose's head was whirling with all the information. 'I—not at all, Lady Ramsay.'

'Oh, Jane, please! We are family.'

'Jane,' Rose answered carefully. She remembered Jane's letter, how it had asked for her help with the children, especially in teaching them music, but it felt like she was being welcomed at Barton as another guest. 'Are the children to make an appearance before dinner?'

'We have to do our songs!' William declared. 'We've been practising them so much, Mother.'

Jane laughed again, and ruffled her son's dark hair. 'I know, my darling, we have heard you. Yes, the children may come down for a while, and as a special treat William and Eleanor can dine with us tonight as it will be very informal. We have to choose the King of the Bean, after all.'

Eleanor clasped Rose's hand and whispered an explanation. 'The King of the Bean is the one who finds the bean in the special cake at dinner tonight and then they will rule over what we do for the rest of the festivities!'

'Oh, I see,' Rose answered. 'Like the Lord of Misrule?'

'Only not as wild, I hope,' Jane said.

'Well, I think it all sounds merry indeed,'

said Rose. 'What time should I have them prepared to come downstairs, then, Jane?'

Jane waved her hand. 'The nursemaids will see to all that. Just come down with them when you're ready. We'll just be a small, cosy party tonight, with Emma and her family, and the vicar and his wife. Oh, and the St George brothers! I am sure you remember Harry and Charles. I was so happy to persuade them to join us this holiday, they seem intent on becoming hermits over at Hilltop.'

'The—the St Georges?' Rose whispered, feeling her cheeks turn warm as she was caught by surprise. Of course she had thought— feared—she might see Harry St George that holiday, as their home was so near Barton, but she hadn't expected to hear his name quite so soon, before she could prepare herself.

'You've gone all pink, Miss Parker,' Eleanor whispered.

'It—it must be warm in here,' she answered faintly.

Luckily, she was saved from answering further by the arrival of an older lady in stiff black silk, keys jangling at her waist from an old-fashioned chatelaine.

'This is Hannah, our dear housekeeper who has been at Barton for ever,' Jane said. 'She will see you to your room. You must take all the time you need to rest before you take on my wee monsters.'

'Mama!' Eleanor protested. 'Miss Parker will think we are most unruly.'

Rose laughed, pushing away thoughts of Harry as she tried to remember what she was really there for—the children and their music. 'Indeed I will not. You seem entirely ladylike to me, Lady Eleanor.'

'If you'll follow me, then, Miss Parker,' Hannah said, as Jane took her children's hands and led them into the drawing room. 'You've been given the yellow room, it's near to the nursery.'

'Of course.' Rose followed the housekeeper up the stairs and down a long corridor, past closed doors and a few open ones where maids bustled about preparing the rooms for their guests. Her own chamber was close to the end of the hall and when Hannah opened the door she saw it was small but lovely. The white-painted bed was covered with a yellow-satin counterpane and draped with pale yellow and green striped silk, as was the small dressing table where a maid was already laying out her toiletries. A fire burned merrily in the little white-marble grate and her trunk was placed near a small desk and yellow-cushioned chair.

'What a lovely space,' she exclaimed. She put down her bonnet as she studied the view out the window, a long landscape of drive and trees, the stone fountain and flowerbeds. She could see for miles; could see anyone making their approach to the house.

'Hmmph,' Hannah said, twitching the curtains into place. 'I will make sure hot water for washing and some tea is sent up. Be sure to let the maids know if you require anything else.'

'I don't think I could possibly need anything else, thank you, Hannah,' Rose answered. A chamber all to herself, with no Aunt Sylvia constantly ringing her summoning bell? It sounded most luxurious.

She glanced again out the window and remembered what Jane had said about the St

Georges and their home nearby. She wondered whimsically if the chimneys she could barely glimpse in the distance belonged to them. Or maybe it was the ruins of the old castle where Arabella once hid her treasure, the story she had once shared with Harry, so long ago?

'Don't be so silly,' she told herself, and pulled the curtains closed. She was there to teach music and that was all. The silly, fanciful girl she had once allowed herself to be for one night so long ago had no place in the world any longer.

Chapter Five

'Will you have some mulled cider, Miss Parker? Lady Ramsay says it is most warming on a cold day,' the stern housekeeper Hannah said as she waited outside the drawing room, holding out a tray laden with tiny crystal glasses filled with ruby-red liquid. Rose had bathed and changed as quickly as she could, but it seemed the party had already begun. She could hear loud laughter from the room, the clink of heavy crystal goblets.

Liquid courage—just what she needed, Rose thought with a laugh. She needed to steel her nerves to face the crowd, especially one that contained Captain St George. 'Thank you very much.' She gratefully took a glass. It was warm through her glove and smelled of rich spices and fine red claret. It smelled exactly like Christmas.

'Her ladyship and the other guests are in the drawing room,' Hannah said, gesturing to the half-open door behind her.

The other guests? Including Harry St George? She hadn't been able to cease thinking about him since she heard he would be there. She could feel her cheeks turning warm again and worried that if they were too pink others would surely notice, as little Lady Eleanor had earlier.

'Am I the last to arrive?' she asked as she tried not to gulp down more of the wine. At Aunt Sylvia's house, the strongest drink was watered sherry and then only when the vicar called. She didn't want to get too giddy before she faced Captain St George again.

'No, Miss Parker. Several others are still dressing, I believe,' Hannah answered, with a disdainful sniff that revealed exactly what she thought of such laggards. 'Some have only just arrived and I believe the St George brothers are still above stairs as well.'

Rose smiled in relief. 'Thank you, Hannah. I will just join the guests, then.' She put her now-empty glass back on the tray and made her way towards the half-open doors of the drawing room. She could hear laughter and the hum of conversation, the faint strains of someone playing the harp, and it made her determined to enjoy her Christmas as well. It would all end much too soon.

Just like the hall and the bedrooms above stairs, the drawing room of Barton Park had been transformed under Jane's care into a space that was stylish, grand and cosy all at the same time. From the warmth of the white and yellow striped silk wallpaper to the flowered cushions of the deep chairs and sofas, to the fire that blazed in the white marble grate and the gold-framed landscape paintings, everything was warm and welcoming.

Rose marvelled, too, at the beautiful holiday decorations. Elaborate swags of greenery tied with red and green bows looped around the picture frames and formed into wreaths above the windows that looked out on to the chilly winter evening where snow was starting down in delicate, lacy flurries. Blue and white Chinese vases on their marble stands were filled with holly branches heavy with red berries and round kissing boughs of mistletoe and streamers hung in every doorway. The warm air smelled sweetly of cinnamon and cloves, spicy and sweet all at the same time.

The crowd gathered around the harp looked just as ready for the holiday spirit as the decorations were, a kaleidoscope of bright, jewel-like velvets and satins. They all sipped at the spiced wine, or sang along as Emma played the harp in an ever-so-slightly off-key version of 'I Saw Three Ships'.

Rose smiled at the scene, at the noise and happy chaos of it all. It had been so long since she saw such merriment around her. Yet it made her feel a bit nervous as well.

She smoothed the simple chignon of her hair, the skirt of her second-best grey silk dress, and hoped she would fit in with such a crowd. She also wished she had worn her spectacles, so faces wouldn't be *quite* so fuzzy. She narrowed her eyes to scan the figures around the harp and to her relief she saw that Hannah had been right—none of them seemed to be Captain St George.

'Rose! There you are,' Jane cried, rising

from the sofa where she sat with two other guests. She wore a gown of deep forest-green satin, but Rose was happy to see the lines were simple, so she didn't feel quite so shabby. Jane's dark hair was tied back with a green and gold bandeau and her only jewellery was a pair of pearl drop earrings. She quickly fetched two glasses from a footman's tray, and hurried over to offer one to Rose. 'Hasn't the weather turned quite beastly? Almost everyone has already arrived, but I think we still expect a few others. I do hope they hurry, as the roads will be quite impassable soon.'

Rose sipped carefully at the wine, hoping it wouldn't go to her head like the last glass. She surveyed the crowd over the crystal rim, not sure how many others could possibly fit into Barton's cosy drawing room. 'Are you expecting very many more, Lady Ra—Jane?'

'Oh, just the Smythes, who are Emma's sister-in-law and her husband, and Lady Fallon. Perhaps you remember her as Miss Helen Layton? She is a widow now.'

Of course Rose remembered the beautiful Miss Layton and how she took Captain

St George's arm so intimately all those years ago. 'I—yes, of course.' She took another sip of wine. 'Barton does look so lovely dressed for the holiday. I can't remember a Christmas so festive.'

Jane laughed. 'Oh, I do hope it is. We're all in need of a lovely, old-fashioned Christmas. We'll have games later, of course, some snapdragon and hide-and-seek, and dancing. I've also arranged a Christmas Day ball and invited all the neighbours.'

The drawing room door opened again, and Rose turned with a smile—only to freeze when she saw it was Harry St George who stood there, along with his brother.

Charles St George was handsome, to be sure, and most fashionably dressed in a blue velvet coat and elaborately tied cravat, but it was Harry she could not look away from. She had heard he was wounded in battle, but not to what extent. He wore a patch over his left eye, and a long, raised reddish-purple scar arced down his cheek. It made Rose's heart ache to think of the pain he must have suffered with it all—and somehow it made him even more handsome than he had been the last time they met.

She swallowed hard and turned away, trying to compose herself before she had to speak to him. She did not want to make a fool of herself in front of him and on her very first day at Barton, too!

Jane came to her rescue. 'Rose, dear, could you favour us with a song at the pianoforte? Nothing makes a holiday merrier than a fine carol!'

'Of course,' Rose said quickly. At the instrument, she could busy herself with the music, which was always a refuge. She hurried to the pianoforte and raised the lid as she tried to decide what to play. It was a very fine instrument indeed, better even than Aunt Sylvia's, and would make an excellent hiding place indeed.

She trailed her fingers over the keys and launched into 'The First Noel'. It was a good enough start to the holidays.

'I do hope I won't be sorry you persuaded me to come to this party, Charlie,' Harry muttered as he studied the crowd gathered in Jane's drawing room. He had avoided such noise since his return from battle, and the loud laughter almost made him want to go back to the silence of his room once more.

Charles laughed and snatched up two glasses of spicy-scented wine from the nearest tray. He handed one to Harry and tossed back the other. 'You agreed that a holiday away from Hilltop would do us both some good. Why not enjoy it, Brother?'

'Harry! Charlie! How lovely to see you,' he heard Jane call out. She emerged from the crowd, a vision of Christmas herself in forest-green and gold. She kissed their cheeks, smiling, and only a flicker of her lashes showed she noticed Harry's scars, his eye patch. 'I am so sorry I wasn't able to greet you when you arrived. I do hope your chambers are satisfactory?'

'When is your hospitality less than perfect, Jane?' Charles said.

'I do want people to be comfortable and, well, happy for the holidays.' She took their arms and led them to a nearby table, where a plan of the dining table was set with small white cards. Their backs were to the crowd, but nothing could disguise the loud singing, the beautiful playing of the pianoforte. Harry found it most distracting, and comforting, to have such familiar diversions. The song was lovely.

'You see, Charlie,' Jane said. 'You are quite near Mrs Anson, the lovely young widow who manages Emma's bookshop for her. She was asking about you just last week. She is also very interested in travel and I do think you have met once or twice before?'

Charles frowned. 'Mrs Anson?' He sounded rather confused. Harry wondered if this young, bookshop-managing widow did not quite fit into Charles's stated heiress scheme. 'I'm not sure I'm quite, er, interested in romance this holiday, Jane.'

'Are you not?' Jane said, teasingly nudging his shoulder. 'Are you sure you are feeling quite well?'

'If matchmaking is your aim for the holiday,' Charles said with a mischievous wink, 'you should turn your attention to my brother.'

'Really?' Jane looked up at Harry with far too much intrigue and delight in her smile for his comfort.

'Jane,' he said warningly. 'Remember what a tease Charlie can be?'

'But ladies so love a war hero!' Jane studied her chart and nudged a card around. 'Lady Fallon is expected, you know, though I fear she has not yet arrived. I am sure you do remember her.'

Of course he remembered Helen and how she had married someone else—and was quite right to do so. They would never have suited in the end. 'Like my brother, I have no interest in romance this Christmas, Jane,' he said cautiously.

'Ah, well, just as you like,' she said with a bright smile. The door opened and Jane's children appeared, accompanied by their nurse and luckily distracting Jane from any matchmaking thoughts for the moment. 'Hello, my darlings! Have you come to sing for us?'

Harry was more relieved than he would have ever expected to see a group of carolling children. He reached for another glass of wine and looked for a quiet corner to retreat to. He turned—and found himself facing Miss Rose Parker, who had just got up from the pianoforte.

She was just as lovely as she had been all those years ago, slender and pale with a faint flush to her cheeks that brought to mind her name—Rose. Her brown hair was twisted up into a plain knot at the nape of her neck, held with a small silver comb that was her only adornment. It matched the light grey of her gown, enlivened only by a narrow edge of pink ribbon.

Her eyes sparkled and they widened as she glimpsed him there. She glanced over her shoulder, as if she would leave, but the crowd pressed too close.

He remembered their dance so long ago, as if it was in another life altogether, but one he could barely glimpse again, like a sunrise on the horizon. If she was not entirely repelled by his new looks.

'Miss Parker,' he said with a bow. 'How wonderful to see you again and looking so well.'

She dipped into a curtsy and as she rose she didn't quite met his gaze. Her gloved hands twitched at her skirts.

'And you, Captain St George,' she said. 'I'm happy you were able to join us for Christmas. Have you been home long?'

'Not long at all. I was in hospital in Italy for a time and the journey home was slower than I would have liked. All those muddy roads.'

Her eyes widened. 'Oh, no! It sounds quite appalling.'

Harry made himself laugh. He had to forget battle now, forget his lost friends. This was what he needed to focus on now. Being at home, doing his duty. 'Not at all. If one must be in hospital, Italy is the place to do it. The best wine and food far better than I've had in English camps. It was almost like a spa-town holiday.'

Rose shook her head, her lips twitching as if she tried not to laugh. She did look directly at him now and didn't seem to notice his patch, his scars at all. Her smile was just the same as it had been all those years ago. 'I'm not sure it was *quite* spa-like, but it does seem to have done wonders for your health.'

'So it has. I hope your own family is well, your mother and sister.'

'Oh, yes, very well. Mama is settled in her own cottage and Lily is married now, with two little ones.'

Harry suddenly wondered with a pang if Rose herself was also married, if her gloves hid a ring. 'And yourself, Miss Parker?'

'Me? I live with my aunt, Mrs Pemberton, as her companion. Jane asked if I could come here for the holiday to teach her children some music and I was glad to be able to visit Barton again.' One of the children cried out and a nursemaid appeared with a crowd of children. They were all clad in their Christmas best, taking in the crowd with wide eyes. 'I should go. Duty calls.'

'It was lovely to see you again, Miss Parker,' he said quickly, before she could run away.

She smiled in a way which seemed both shy and hopeful. Or maybe he was the one feeling hopeful in that moment. 'And you, Captain.'

She hurried off to lead the children to the pianoforte set near to the fireplace. Rose sat down on the bench again, her plain grey skirts draping gracefully around her. The children gathered close.

'What should we sing, then?' Rose asked cheerfully.

'What about "The Holly and the Ivy"?' Jane said, sorting through a stack of sheet music. 'We are all going on a greenery-gathering expedition tomorrow.'

'A very good choice indeed,' Rose said. She took off her gloves and tripped her fingertips lightly over the keys before she nodded at the children and launched into the song. Everyone else in the room gathered close to listen and Harry edged towards the door, out of the crowd.

But he couldn't escape yet. The door opened again to admit a latecomer. Harry was startled to see it was Helen Fallon, swathed in red velvet and glossy sables, rubies twinkling in her ears. Just like Miss Parker, she had not aged since Harry last saw her, perhaps seemed even younger. More glowing. So bright, in fact, she looked as if she would burn from it.

'Oh, dear, am I late?' she cried, handing her sable muff and velvet gloves to a footman and reaching for a glass of champagne on a tray. 'So bad of me, missing a party.' She glimpsed him over the edge of her glass and slowly lowered it. Her brilliant smile faded. 'Harry.'

'Hello, Helen,' he answered. How long he had known her; how their childhoods were so entwined. Yet it felt like looking at a stranger. 'How beautiful you look.'

'Hardly aged a day,' Charles said, coming up behind them to take his own glass of wine. 'Here we all are again together. Just like old times, yes?'

The sound of the old carol sounded around them, a merry counterpoint to the sudden sense of unreality Harry felt.

'Just like,' Helen said wryly.

'Please, excuse me, Helen,' Harry said. 'I have an errand. I shall see you at dinner.'

'Yes, I want to hear all about what you've been doing,' she answered. 'All your adventures…'

Harry glanced at her fine pelisse. 'They can't have been as adventurous as your own life, I'm sure.'

Helen laughed. 'London? It's dull as tombs. At least here there is this lovely champagne.'

Harry bowed and made his way out of the drawing room. He heard the music swelling behind him and Charlie and Helen laughing together. But he knew that the past, the past they had once shared as children, was gone.

He only wished he could have spent more time talking with Miss Parker, standing in her gentle presence as the rest of the world swirled noisily around them.

Chapter Six

"'As I lay on Yoolis Night, Alone in my long-ynge, I thought I saw a well faire sight, A maid hir child rockynge.'"

'That was beautifully played, Eleanor,' Rose said with a smile as the girl finished her song at the pianoforte in the morning room. Rose had been most glad of the excuse of a music lesson to avoid breakfast with the other guests. She had seen the way Lady Fallon looked at Captain St George last night and it had made her feel strange and discombobulated, as if she wasn't quite supposed to be there. She wasn't sure she could face watching them at breakfast as well. And she was, after all, at Barton to teach music.

But the music lesson had proved most enjoyable. Rose had always been able to lose herself in a song, to pour out her emotions into the notes, and it seemed young Lady Eleanor was the same way. Her sensitivity to the song, the easy way her small fingers played over the keys, was a delight.

Eleanor smiled shyly. 'Do you truly think so, Miss Parker? I always have such trouble here…'

'That is where you must change chords like this,' Rose said, showing her on the keyboard. 'It merely takes a bit of practice. But you have something much rarer—the ability to capture the very mood of a song.'

Eleanor nodded. 'So, when I am sad or frightened, I should play a happy song? To help me remember something lovely, like a warm summer's day?'

'Exactly so!' Rose exclaimed. 'I often do that myself.'

Eleanor gave her a long, questioning glance. 'Are you often unhappy, Miss Parker?'

'Not at all, my dear,' Rose answered gently. 'Music is a celebration at happy times as well as an escape at sad ones, you know. Just like now, at Christmas. We must rehearse more carols later this afternoon, something to dance to, perhaps?'

'Rehearsing!' William scoffed. He lay on his stomach on the pale blue carpet, pushing around a tiny carriage and horses. It seemed music did not interest him as much as it did his sister. 'That sounds very dull. We know the songs well enough. Who can sit still that long, singing one line over and over?'

Rose had to laugh; he sounded so much as Lily had when they were children and she was too impatient to practise. 'What would you rather do, then, William? Read your geography lessons?'

'We could tell you about the treasure!' he said eagerly. His sat up, his carriage forgotten for the moment.

'The treasure?' Rose asked. She wondered if it was the same one that had entranced her and Lily when they were children.

'It's just an old story,' Eleanor said. 'Cousin Beatrice likes to tell us about how she went searching for it once, when she was our age. She hurt herself and Aunt Emma had to go find her. It's why we're not allowed near the old castle ruins on Uncle David's estate.'

'We would be much more careful if we were the ones searching!' William said. 'I'm sure it's there some place. It would make a splendid Christmas surprise for Mama and Aunt Emma if we found it.'

'Arabella's old treasure?' Rose said, falling into their enthusiasm. 'My sister and I used to like that tale, too.'

'Was Arabella the lady from a long time ago?' William asked.

'When Charles I was king and they wanted him to go,' Eleanor added. 'This lady was in love with one of the king's own knights…'

'And she hid a treasure for him in the old castle, so they could be together one day!' said William. 'But he died and she never returned for it, so it is out there some place.'

'It does certainly sound romantic,' Rose said, finding herself rather sorry for this long-ago couple, kept apart by the cold realities of the world. 'But I am sure your parents are quite right not to let you go climbing about old ruins by yourself.'

'I do think it's terribly sad Arabella never got to marry her true love,' Eleanor said with a sigh. 'I would only ever marry a man I loved madly, as Mama and Aunt Emma have done.'

'Girls are so silly in that way,' William said.

Rose laughed. 'Why will *you* marry, then, William?'

'I don't know. Because I find a pretty girl some day, I suppose. Her portrait will have to go in the gallery of countesses, you know,' he said grandly.

Rose laughed even louder. She had known teaching children music would be better than serving tea to Aunt Sylvia all day, but she hadn't realised it would be quite so amusing. 'Very wise of you.'

Eleanor glanced up at her. 'Why have you not married, Miss Parker? You are certainly pretty.'

Rose smiled at her and pushed her spectacles up her nose. She remembered Lady Fallon, with her beautiful gown and shining hair, everyone watching her as she laughed. Who would notice someone like Rose after that? And she knew marriage didn't often turn out as well as it had for her sister and her cousins. 'I haven't found someone to fall madly in love with yet.'

Eleanor gave a sad-looking frown and gently touched Rose's hand. 'I am sure you will, though, and very soon.'

'In the meantime, perhaps you might search for treasure with us?' William said hopefully.

Rose shook her head. 'I have been hired to teach you music, so I think we should go over these Christmas carols again. Something jolly, maybe—a dance?'

William reluctantly joined them at the pianoforte bench, but they had barely made it through their next song before there was a knock at the door. Jane hurried in, clad in a fur-trimmed pelisse and hat, a matching fur muff in her hand.

'Mama!' the children cried and ran to hug her.

'How is your lesson progressing, then, Rose?' Jane said as she hugged her children back. 'Are they prodigies yet?'

'They are excellent pupils,' Rose answered.

'Very good. I think that deserves a reward, then, don't you? We're all going out to collect more greenery in the park and since you have been such good children you may come with us,' Jane said. As the children cheered, she told them to go tell the nursemaid to fetch their coats.

William shouted out with happiness and dashed away, Eleanor following with one small, wistful glance behind her at the pianoforte. Rose started to tidy the musical sheets, already missing their company.

'You must come, too, Rose,' Jane said.

Go out—and see Harry St George again? 'Oh, no...'

'I absolutely insist! You are obviously a wonder with my children, I haven't seen them so well behaved in an age,' Jane said. 'And it's a lovely day outside; the sun is shining, though it's a bit chilly. I don't think we'll have many more days of such weather.'

Rose glanced out the window; she did have to agree it looked quite nice out, the pale sunlight shimmering on yesterday's dusting of snow. Surely there would be so many people there she wouldn't even find herself alone with Harry. She smiled and hurried off to find her pelisse and hat.

The rest of the party was already gathered in the front drive when Rose hurried to join them. Various carts and carriages waited, equipped with warm blankets, picnic baskets, as well as tools for cutting green boughs once they were found.

For a moment, she stood in the shadows of the doorway, just watching the bright scene before her. At Aunt Sylvia's house they seldom had company at all, except for the elderly vicar for tea, and at her mother's cottage they'd had no time or money for parties. This felt like a whole different world, the swirling brightness of velvet pelisses and caped greatcoats, the sound of laughter. She wasn't sure she belonged there.

She saw a quieter cart near the end of the row and started to turn towards it, to remain unobtrusive and watchful. But Emma Marton suddenly grabbed her hand and drew her into the very midst of the chattering throng, gathering her close.

'Miss Parker, I do believe there is a seat here,' she heard a deep, rich voice say, and turned to see Captain St George holding out his hand to her with a half-smile. In the sunlight, his scars looked more evident, yet that smile was as handsome as ever. *Too* handsome for her peace of mind.

Rose glanced around, but there was nowhere else to sit. *Don't be such a ninny,* she told herself sternly. Yes, he was an attractive man, and, yes, talking to him last night had made her feel things she never had before. Most confusing things, such as—a girlish desire to laugh. The exhilarating sense of being *seen*, of being heard, of being free of all the caution and responsibility, to be just a young lady talking to a handsome man, if only for a moment.

All those things *had* happened and it felt like a dream. Yet this was in the clear, cold light of day and she was a sensible, grown woman. A woman with many responsibilities. Surely she could not now make a giggling, silly fool out of herself.

He curled the outstretched fingers of his gloved hand and his smile widened, as if he could read her thoughts. His uncovered eye, so very blue, gleamed like a summer sky.

Oh, yes, she thought wryly. She could be a giggling, silly fool after all.

But she didn't have to show it to everyone. She smiled back and took his hand to let him help her on to the cart. She sat down beside him on the narrow bench, demurely arranging her skirts around herself. A few other people clambered up with them, and she glimpsed Lady Fallon climbing into the carriage ahead of theirs, helped by Charles St George. She watched Harry from under the brim of her fur-trimmed bonnet.

'I hope you slept well enough after last night's festivities, Miss Parker,' he said. 'I saw William racing through the hall this morning and he said he was late for your music lesson. I think he was stealing bacon from the dining-room sideboard.'

Rose laughed, more at ease with his light tone. 'Oh, yes, it all went quite well. Barton Park is very comfortable and the children most attentive to their lessons—once they are there. Lady Eleanor in particular is very talented.' She peeked up at him from beneath the brim of her plain grey bonnet. He smiled at her again and she suddenly felt so light, so wonderfully giddy.

'I remember from our last meeting, as well as last night, that you quite enjoy music, Miss

Parker,' he said. 'Jane says that she's lucky to have a lady of your rare talent instructing her children.'

Rose felt her cheeks turn warm under his praise and looked away as the cart jolted in motion. 'I have no more talent than most ladies who are made to practise their pianoforte and harp from their childhood,' she said with a laugh. 'But, yes, I do enjoy it, very much. When I have the chance to play. My Aunt Sylvia does like things to be—quiet.'

The cart jolted around a corner, following the line of carriages before it in their jolly little caravan. Rose was not prepared for the sudden motion and fell against Harry's shoulder. He caught her against him and for an instant she felt all of herself pressed against him. She sat up straighter, feeling her cheeks grow embarrassingly warm again, and she was all too aware of his strength pressed so close to her.

In the open carriage ahead of theirs, Charles St George stood up and started to lead everyone in a rousing chorus of 'We Wish You a Merry Christmas'. The riders around Rose and Harry soon took up the tune and they were surrounded by the wondrous sounds of the season as they jolted and jounced over the frosty lanes into the wooded part of the park. Charles almost toppled over on to Lady Fallon.

'I do not think Barton could ever be described as *quiet*,' Harry remarked wryly.

Rose laughed. 'No, indeed. Aunt Sylvia would quite hate it. Your brother does seem to take his role as Lord of Misrule for the holiday most seriously.'

Harry smiled and Rose had the sense it was something rather rare for him, smiling. She found herself wanting to make him do it again, to laugh even. 'Charles would be King of the Revels all the time if he could.'

'He sounds like my sister, Lily. She does love a good party.'

'The curate's wife?' Harry said, his tone surprised.

Rose laughed again. 'You must not let that fool you. She does take her parish duties and her children very seriously, but she still loves a dance or a practical joke more than anyone I have ever known. When we were children, she would gallop up and down the stairs and pretend to be a pony whenever she could!'

'And you, Miss Parker? Did you concoct such games when you were a girl?'

Rose studied the scenery around them, the trees growing thicker, the shadows darker, as she thought about her girlhood with Lily, the sounds of music and laughter that had always echoed around their corridors—until their father died. She turned back to Harry to find him watching her intently, as if he could read her wistfulness.

'The world is different for an eldest child, is it not, Miss Parker?' he said.

'Is it, Captain?' She thought more of her childhood, of the times she had pulled Lily back from disaster. 'I had never thought of it thus, but so it seems. Someone must keep it all from falling to bits, I suppose.'

'Or put it back together when it does,' he answered, so softly she wasn't sure she'd heard him.

Before she could answer, could tell him of how things had fallen apart when her father died, the cart lurched to a halt in a large clearing surrounded by a circle of trees.

'Very well, everyone,' Charles cried, still Lord of Misrule, 'I command you all to go out and find as much greenery as possible to deck the halls of Barton tonight. The winner will have the first glass from the wassail bowl!'

A great cheer went up and everyone scattered into the woods like a flock of brightly coloured birds. Harry held out his hand to help Rose down, but when she stumbled on the step he swiftly caught her around the waist before she could fall. She gasped with surprise at the sparkling jolt of pleasure his touch gave her.

As he slowly lowered her to her feet, Rose wished she didn't have to let him go. Didn't have to keep her feet planted firmly on the plain, practical ground, as she always did. The Christmas spirit was taking her over.

'Th-thank you, Captain St George,' she said, wishing her voice did not sound quite so breathless. 'So clumsy of me.'

'Not at all. I'm afraid I must beg *your* assistance now, Miss Parker.'

'My assistance?'

'Yes. I see a patch of holly over there just begging to be a mantelpiece decoration, but my depth perception is not—quite what it was.' He gestured to the dark cloth over his eye.

'Oh, of course!' Rose cried, embarrassed she had forgotten his injuries. The truth was, after the first shock when they met again last night, she had barely noticed his scars. He was still much too attractive for her peace of mind. 'I am quite sure that between us we can defeat the holly and bring it home in triumph.'

As he offered her his arm, she glimpsed Lady Fallon's red pelisse through the trees, just ahead of them. She smiled up at Harry and took his arm to make their way between the thick wood, chattering easily about inconsequential matters such as the cold weather, favourite Christmas songs from their childhood holidays, and places they had seen— many for Harry, few for Rose. A chilly breeze swept around the bare branches, making the voices of the others a mere murmur, but pale sunlight struggled down on to their heads through the lacy patterns.

'And where else have you travelled, Captain St George?' she asked as she paused to clip a clump of low-hanging mistletoe, pearly with white berries.

'To Switzerland and Austria, many places in Italy,' he said, as casually as if he'd said Kent or Brighton.

'How lucky you are to have seen such things,' she said. 'I have never even been to Bath!'

He gave her a smile. 'Bath is overrated, I assure you, Miss Parker. As is Italy.'

Rose gazed around them at the quiet trees, the silent, pale sky. 'This must all seem so dull to you after all you have seen. A plain English country Christmas.'

He turned to study her for a moment, his gaze unreadable. She turned away with a blush. 'Oh, Miss Parker. An English country Christmas is one of the loveliest things imaginable. This quiet is astounding.'

'Of course it would be,' she answered softly. 'I have only read of battle and can barely imagine the noise and confusion of it all. I'm glad you have returned safely home.'

He smiled down at her warmly. 'I see you do understand, Miss Parker. So few do, even my brother. They think once it's over it is forgotten. And it's not a memory I wish to dwell upon, especially on such a lovely day.'

Rose nodded. 'Shall we conquer that holly, then? I see some with particularly luscious red berries right over there.'

She laughed and took his arm to make their way to the holly bush. It was indeed a lovely one, dark green against the frosty ground like diamonds and rubies. She held the branches high and still as he sawed them off to fill their baskets. She could hear the laughter of the others caught on the wind, could smell the crisp, warm scent of him against the cold snow and the greenery.

'This is quite nice,' she said. 'It does remind me of Christmases when I was a child and Lily and I would help our parents find decorations for the house. It smelled of evergreen then and we were always singing. My father would read us old holiday poems every night. How merry it was!'

He nodded, but he looked solemn as he finished gathering the last of the branches. 'It sounds delightful indeed.'

'Did you and your brother not do such things for Christmas at your house?'

'Christmas was not much celebrated at Hilltop, I'm afraid, so I'm learning it as I go this year. My father preferred quiet at all times and my mother usually went to visit friends in London, though she did like a bit of decoration around the house.'

'Oh,' Rose whispered, her heart suddenly aching for him. He smiled as he spoke, as if it was not a thing of much consequence, yet she heard the sombre touch of wistfulness behind the words. She couldn't help but picture two lonely little boys, left alone at the darkest time of the year without the Yule candles to brighten things. 'I am sorry.'

'Not at all. Charlie and I would be left alone to do naughty things like toast cheese by the fire, which we were never usually allowed to do.'

Rose laughed. 'Toasted cheese *is* a thing to look forward to, I must say. Aunt Sylvia would never allow it.'

He studied her from beneath the brim of his hat. 'What is it like at your Aunt Sylvia's house?'

Rose thought about the drawing room, cluttered with old *objets* and closed around with heavy velvet curtains. 'Not so terrible, really. It's not as if I'm mining coal or some such thing. Mostly I read to her and fetch tea and shawls, and listen as she bemoans the ways of the world. We are apparently in quite a shocking state, you know, compared with how things were in her own youth.'

He laughed. 'So my father often said. I think I remember reading Plato saying the young people of his own day were becoming shockingly rude. By the time any nephews or nieces of mine are grown, who knows what horrors we shall face?'

Rose noticed he'd said 'nephews and nieces', not sons and daughters. Did he not hope for such things as a family, then? She wondered what horrors had taken such expectations from him and she wanted to touch his hand in sympathy, as Lady Eleanor had for her earlier that morning. But he gave her another smile, and in that smile, just for an instant, she glimpsed the man she had danced with all those years ago, in another life. The man whose kindness and handsome looks had fuelled her silly dreams for far too long. Whatever he'd seen and done in battle had carved the man with such sadness as well as outward scars, yet she saw the man she'd known was still inside somewhere.

'Well, I think I am about to do something shockingly naughty,' she whispered.

He leaned closer with a glint in his eye. 'I can't wait to see what that might be, Miss Parker.'

'I see a lovely little cluster of mistletoe up there and every house decorated for the holidays *must* have plenty of mistletoe for kissing boughs. I'm going to climb up there to fetch it.'

'Climb the tree?' he said doubtfully. 'Miss Parker, I don't think….'

Before he could stop her, Rose ran to the tree and found a foothold in the rough bark. She reached up and grabbed a thick branch. 'Lily and I used to climb trees all the time, when we were children. I'm sure I remember how.'

He frowned and rushed over to her, his arms out as if he was afraid she would fall. 'It could be dangerous.'

'Not as dangerous as riding into battle like

you, Captain,' she answered and kept pulling herself upwards.

She felt a warm touch on her leg and looked down to find he was ready to catch her at an instant's notice. Somehow, just knowing he was there gave her more confidence.

She grabbed at the cluster of mistletoe and snapped it off. As she clambered back down, the toe of her boot caught on her hem and she felt herself falling with an instant of cold panic.

Before she could hit the frost-frozen ground, Harry caught her, holding her high for an instant above the rest of the world. Breathless, Rose held on to him and felt safer than she had in a very long time.

'Thank you, Captain,' she said. 'It seems you have saved me yet again.'

'I must find something useful to do in my new homebound life,' he answered. 'Rescuing fair maidens seems as fine a cause as any.'

Rose laughed as he lowered her to her feet. She found she didn't want to let him go at all; she had to make herself stand back and smile. 'You're quite good at it. And look at our mistletoe! Quite pretty, indeed, and not a single berry lost.'

She suddenly heard other voices, calling out and laughing, and she remembered they were not alone in the fairy-tale woods. Her small dream was shattered, like the icicles on the trees around them, and she stepped back from him.

'There you are, Rose,' Jane called. 'I think it's time for our luncheon, don't you? We've all been working much too hard! Oh, look at how much holly you've gathered, how marvellous.'

As Jane took her arm and led her away, still happily chattering, Rose glanced back at Harry.

Lady Fallon had gone to him and taken his arm, and he replied to whatever she had said to him. Rose's throat tightened, but she made herself turn away and nod and smile at Jane. The day suddenly stretched very long before her.

Rose Parker sat the other end of the long luncheon table, with several laughing, chattering people between them, but Harry was aware of her at every moment. Aware of her soft smiles, the graceful movement of her hand as she raised her glass, and the quiet, sweet happiness that seemed to radiate around her like a pink, sunset cloud.

Yes—that was what she had, what he had never possessed—quiet sweetness, a pleasure in the moment. It was intoxicating after years of noise and chaos in the army.

He thought of that moment in the forest, with the snowy silence all around them and Rose looking up at him. He had wanted to take her into his arms more than he had ever wanted anything else, longed for it with a palpable hunger that took him entirely by surprise.

'…don't you think, Harry?' Helen, who was seated to his right, said. Her laughing voice pushed him out of his dream world and into the reality of the cold winter morning, of a footman pouring wine into his glass and Helen laying a light hand on his arm.

He glanced down into her smiling eyes, those beautiful sky-blue eyes of his old friend, the woman he'd even once thought of marrying. And all he could think of was

Rose, her cheeks pink in the cold forest, her smile.

'...*should marry an heiress,*' he heard Charlie say in his mind. *'Do his duty—rescue Hilltop.'*

'I'm sorry, Helen, I fear I was wool-gathering,' he said.

She tilted her head, the feathers of her fashionable headpiece waving lightly. Her gaze flickered over his ruined face and then away. 'Charlie was just telling me about how Hilltop needs a lady's opinion on its furnishings. Perhaps I could advise you?'

Harry almost laughed as he thought of Hilltop, its roof slates crumbling, its floors cracking. Refurnishing was far down the list at the moment. 'I don't think it's quite ready for visitors.'

Helen laughed and reached for her wineglass. 'I am hardly a visitor. I remember being there so often as a child it almost seemed like a second home.'

Charles gave Harry a long, solemn glance over her head. 'We wouldn't know where to start without an educated opinion, would we, Harry?'

'I would so dearly love to see it again,' Helen said with a sigh. 'I am sure that whatever needs fixing there, it is nothing a lady's sure hand could not do. Your father was alone there for so long and a house is not a home without a mistress. A bit of merriment always helps as well.'

'And a new roof wouldn't hurt,' Charlie muttered.

'But such things are surely fixed in a trice!' Helen said. 'Then a bit of redecorating, in modern colours, and it would be just like in our mothers' day. Tell me, Charlie dear, what are the French styles you saw while you were abroad?'

As Charles and Helen talked of colours and satins, Harry finished his wine and thought of that new roof. In Helen's world, such things happened as if by magic. For Hilltop and its tenants—well, it would take a bit more than the wave of a wand.

Chapter Seven

'The boar's head in hand bear I, bedecked in bays and rosemary!'

Rose applauded along with everyone else as the elaborate platter with the traditional boar's head—bright red apple in its mouth and wound with a holly garland—was paraded around the dining room with Charles St George leading the song in his Lord of Misrule role. It was a true traditional Christmas dinner, the table laden with plum cakes and silver wassail bowls, and everyone looked quite merry indeed.

She glanced across the table at Harry. He watched it all with a smile, but it seemed distant, as if he thought of something far away. She wanted to draw him closer, to bring him into their merriment so he forgot all else.

'Oh, Miss Parker, isn't it all so pretty?' Lady Eleanor, seated at Rose's left so she could be guided when it was time for her to sing, said as she watched the firelit scene with wide eyes. She reminded Rose of Lily when they were children, all curls and smiles, and it made her feel wistful to remember.

'Pretty indeed. Much like it must have been here years ago.'

'My father, as you know, was a scholar,' Jane said, listening to her daughter. 'And he always thought the old Christmas traditions were the best. Tonight we have singing, and the wassail bowl, and on Christmas Day and Boxing Day feasts and dancing.'

'And presents?' Eleanor asked.

Jane laughed. 'Small ones, perhaps.'

As plates of roasted boar and cinnamon-spiced apples were passed around the table, Rose thought of the Christmases she had known as a child, with her parents and Lily. They had not been grand, but there had always been singing around the pianoforte, special cakes at tea and her mother's embroidered handkerchiefs as gifts, wrapped around sweets and oranges.

Suddenly, the warm, crowded room seemed to vanish and she was swept up on a chilly wave of homesickness, of missing her mother and sister. She felt so alone in the midst of the noisy crowd and blinked hard to hold back the tears.

She glanced up and found Harry watching her from across the table. He gave her a small, understanding smile, as if he understood what she was thinking, and suddenly she did not feel so very alone.

'Christmas can be a difficult time to remember the past,' he said quietly. 'Whether it be scholarly, or in our own memories.'

'Then we must make new memories,' Jane said. 'William, Eleanor, would you like to sing for us now, my dears?'

The children looked to Rose and she nodded with a smile. No matter what, music, especially when shared with others, was a great refuge. They launched into another version of 'The Boar's Head', their small faces shining with pleasure. They made her forget, too, made her feel like just for a moment she was home again.

'Oh, well done, my dears!' Jane said,

leading the applause. She exchanged proud glances with her husband. 'Rose, you have worked wonders with them.'

Rose was also most proud of her pupils and urged them to make another bow. 'The talent must be there to be worked with, I must say.'

'Will *you* sing something for us, Miss Parker?' Hayden said.

'Oh, yes, do!' Emma cried. 'No one sings as you do.'

Rose slowly stood up, wondering what she should sing, trying not to look at all the people watching her. She closed her eyes and remembered the sad old song her father once sang to her and her sister as they fell asleep at Christmastime.

'"*Lully, lullay, thou little tiny child, Bye-bye, lully, lullay. Lully, lullay, thou little tiny child, Bye-bye, lully, lullay,*"' she sang out.

As she made her way through the verses, a few voices joined her in sweet melancholy.

The words to the old song slowly faded away and Rose felt her homesickness grow in her heart again. Against her will, she found herself looking to Harry again, as if he could offer understanding, as he had earlier when they talked together about past holidays and seemed to be in perfect accord with each other.

He looked as startled as she felt, as if for an instant a mask had dropped away between them and a longing was laid bare. A flash of loneliness, comfort offered and accepted.

Then it was gone, his polite half-smile returned, and applause rang out for the song, breaking the sweet, sad stretch of silence.

'Will you sing for us again?' Jane asked.

Rose shook her head, afraid she would cry if she sang one of the old, familiar songs again. 'Perhaps someone else would grace us?' She glimpsed Lady Fallon from the corner of her eye, a scarlet-satin slipper tapping under her embroidered hem as Jane said,

'Lady Fallon, would you? Rose, perhaps you would join us for a hand of cards?'

Lady Fallon looked startled for an instant before she nodded. 'Oh, yes, of course, though I fear I am quite out of practice!'

Rose gave up the bench to Lady Fallon, who sorted through the music before she launched into a complicated Italian aria. As she sang, Rose sat down and examined her hand of cards, trying to remember how to play piquet. Aunt Sylvia rarely had enough company to make up a four-hand, so Rose's memory of the rules was rather faded. But Jane insisted she would do very well with herself, Emma and Emma's bookseller friend Mrs Anson at the table near the windows.

Lady Fallon's beringed hands flew over the pianoforte keys. Rose saw she was not well practised at her music, but she was very dramatic, drawing people near with her smiling, animated performance—including Harry and Charles, who gathered with the others near the instrument.

'It's quite delightful to see Lady Fallon and the St Georges together again,' Jane said, shuffling the cards. 'It's been too long.'

'Didn't I hear that they were once all great friends?' Mrs Anson asked.

'Oh, yes, their mothers were bosom bows,' Emma said. 'I think there were hopes of Helen and Harry making a match.'

'Really?' Mrs Anson said, her tone surprised. 'But Charles St George is so very handsome, and seems better suited to her—ebullience.'

Jane shrugged, dealing a new hand. 'It all became pointless when Harry went to battle and Lord Fallon came along with his great fortune. But now that Helen is a widow…'

'With all Lord Fallon's gold intact,' Emma said. 'What good such things could do at an estate like Hilltop! It would be lovely to see the old house come alive again.'

'Why?' Rose asked. 'What is amiss with it?'

'Old Mr St George was not the best steward,' Jane said. 'When his wife died, he quite lost all interest in the place. And with Harry and Charlie gone for so long—it was very sad.'

Emma glanced at the group around the pianoforte. 'Yet all can be well now!'

'Hopefully.' Jane glanced out the window, and let out a little glad cry. 'Oh, look, more snow! How delightful. Hayden has been wanting to try his hand at sledding again, as he did when he was a boy. Maybe we can all go tomorrow.'

Rose watched the snow drifting down,

light and lacy, pale against the night sky. It was all so pretty, so peaceful. If only, she thought, all of life could be just that way.

Chapter Eight

How very strange it was, Rose thought, how very alone a person could really feel in a crowd. She felt steadier there, alone for a moment on the chilly terrace as everyone else took a moment from their games to find refreshments, than she had been surrounded by people and gossip about Captain St George and Lady Fallon. The light snowfall fell on her nose and made her laugh.

The glass doors opened behind her, the merest brush against the stone floor, and she turned to see a silhouetted figure against the night sky, the lights from the party behind him. His face was in shadow, but she knew it was Harry. No one else had quite his military bearing.

She felt her cheeks turning warm even in the chilly wind and looked away.

'Oh, I am sorry,' he said when he saw her there. 'I didn't know anyone was here. I was just looking for a—well, a bit of quiet. I'll leave you to your privacy.'

'It's quite all right, Captain,' she answered, hoping he wouldn't leave. 'I also needed some quiet for a moment, but I'm not averse to a bit of company, either.'

'Neither am I, especially when it's so amiable.' He came to stand beside her at the balustrade, leaning his palms on the cold marble. They stared together into the garden, all ghostly under the winter moon. 'Jane's party is very merry, but I'm not quite used to so very many people yet. My brother says I've become a growly old hermit.'

Rose studied him for a moment, his sharp profile against the snow, the sweep of his glossy hair back from his brow. 'I think you would have to grow a much longer beard to be a true hermit. You don't look nearly enough as if you lived in the woods.' They laughed together, and suddenly Rose felt entirely at ease for the first time that evening.

'I do know what you mean. It's so quiet at my aunt's house, I barely know how to make sense of all this noise. It's been a long time since I had a real family Christmas.'

He glanced at her, one brow arched in question. In the night, his scars were invisible. 'Were your childhood Christmases so very merry?'

'Not as grand as this. We usually visited my mother's relatives for New Year, but Christmas was just for us. My parents, my sister, Lily, and me. We would play games, do charades, eat too much pudding. We did have fun.'

'Your father has passed on?'

'Yes, years ago. My mother is still with us. She lives in a cottage near my sister and her family.' She hesitated for a moment, not accustomed to talking about her family. Yet somehow with him, there in the muffling quiet of the snowy night, she felt as if she could say anything. 'My father was something of a gentleman, you see, the grandson of a baron, a good match for my mother with her connection to the Bancrofts, and we had a lovely house with a very pretty garden. Lily and I used to play hide and seek for hours, or go into the attics to read and daydream. But when our father died, we found out he—well, he had debts.'

Harry frowned. 'And that is why you work as companion to your aunt?'

'Yes. Lily was already so fond of her curate and my mother's annuity is not large. Aunt Sylvia is always—interesting. I'm happy to be *here* for the festive season, though. Being with the children reminds me of those times.' She glanced back through the glass doors at the party, the glittering group gathered around the punch bowl, laughing together. Lady Fallon's jewels sparkled in the candle-light and Rose remembered the talk about her old understanding with Harry. 'You said before that yours were not so merry?'

'Not as fun as yours,' he answered with a laugh. 'Charlie and I made do, though. We would play our own games in the nursery and cajole the cook for extra gingersnaps. My father really *was* something of an old hermit, but my mother had a ball each year after New Year's Eve, when she returned from London. Charlie and I would sneak out to watch everyone arrive from the top of the stairs. My mother and her friends were so lovely, all laughing and shimmering in their holiday finery. I think it was the only time of year we really saw her laugh.'

Rose nodded, wondering if Lady Fallon reminded him of those days. 'Perhaps you can have Christmas balls at Hilltop again, now that you're home.'

He gave her a crooked smile. 'I wouldn't be as good at entertaining as Jane and Hayden.'

'But it wouldn't have to be just like this. It could be—family. And books and flowers, treats at breakfast, games after supper. Maybe gathering holly for a wreath or two. The important thing is sharing the holiday.'

His smile faded, but she thought he looked intrigued. 'The way your holidays were as a child?'

Rose nodded. 'Yes, indeed. Christmas can be whatever you want it to be. Whatever you need it to be.'

'I am sure you are quite right.'

She glanced through the doors again and glimpsed Eleanor and William dashing around the room, nearly running into a large vase of ivy and hothouse roses. 'Oh, no, they are meant to be in bed! I should go and gather them up, maybe make them sing another song if they have too much energy.'

To her surprise, he caught her hand in his as she turned away and raised her gloved fingers for a quick kiss. It felt warm and soft through the thin silk. 'Thank you for spending a few moments with me, Miss Parker. You've certainly brought back some memories for me.'

Flustered, Rose dropped a quick curtsy to him. 'Thank *you*, Captain, for keeping me company.'

She hurried back into the drawing room, trying not to look at him, to run back to him. As she slipped back into the party, it was like being dropped into another world entirely, full of noise and heat from the fire and the spicy scent of the wine punch.

Yet even in the warmth, she couldn't help wishing she was back on the chilly terrace, with him.

Chapter Nine

~~~~~~~~~~~~~~~~~~~~

The cold wind snapped at Rose's cheeks and caught at her pelisse, and she laughed as she wondered if this was such a good idea after all. Sledding sounded like such a holiday fun sort of thing to do while cosy next to the fire in Barton, but the reality of it was quite cold indeed!

But Harry was there. She tucked her gloved hands deeper into her old velvet muff, watching him as he built a fire with his brother, Hayden and David Marton, the four of them competing to see who could pile the firewood higher.

He was a fine sight to see indeed, with his dark wool coat stretched taut over his wide shoulders as he stacked the wood. He had taken off his hat and his dark hair gleamed like ebony in the pale sunlight. He laughed at something Charles said, his bright smile breaking through his solemn demeanour. It made the cold day feel suddenly very—warm.

She was glad she had ventured out after all. The real world of daily worries seemed very far away.

She went and sat next to Jane and Emma, where they perched on a fallen log covered by an old blanket. At their feet was a hamper, overflowing with delicacies from the Barton kitchen. As the laughter of the children rang out from the nearby woods where they ran, Emma pulled out gingerbread and almond cakes and candied fruit tarts.

'Oh, sugared plums! And minced pies, salmon sandwiches, even some of the French wine,' Emma exclaimed. 'I have had such a craving for marzipan lately.'

'I feared I was stealing too much from the pantry, but I just had to grab whatever I saw. I dared not stay too long in the kitchen while they're working so hard to prepare for the ball,' Jane said. She poured out spiced wine into heavy pottery goblets. 'Here, Rose, have something fortifying to drink. The wine will warm us.'

'Thank you,' Rose said as she took the goblet. She felt the warmth of the wine through her glove and even better was the warmth of Jane and Emma's friendship. She hadn't realised quite how lonely and quiet her life had become after she left her mother and sister.

As she sipped at the rich, ruby-red drink, she went back to studying Harry. The men had finished building the fire and it snapped merrily as they stood back to watch it, congratulating each other on the fine job.

'Ha!' Jane said with a laugh. 'They act as if they were the first men to discover fire.'

'Better than letting us continue to shiver here,' Emma said.

'Quite right, my dear,' David Marton called to her. 'What would you do without our fire-making skills? Now, can you share some of that wine before we tote these sleds uphill for you?'

The ladies laughed and passed around the spiced wine before Hayden counted the sleds. 'We have enough for almost everyone to pair up, I think. Jane, my dear, shall I steer one for us?'

Jane laughed. 'I am not sure I entirely trust you not to send us into a tree!'

He put his arm around his wife, grinning. 'I have done all right so far, haven't I?'

In the confusion of dividing up the sleds, Rose somehow found herself with Harry. She glanced over her shoulder, half-fearing what she might feel if she was too near him, but everyone else was already making their way up the hill.

She turned back to Harry to find him smiling at her, offering his hand. 'Shall we, Miss Parker?' he said. 'I can't promise to steer us straight, my eyesight is not quite what it was, but I am sure we'll end up some place interesting.'

Rose laughed. Of that, she was quite sure. 'Thank you, Captain St George.' She took his hand and let him help her up the slope of the hill, where he situated their sled to make the downward slide. She perched behind him, her arms around his waist, and closed her eyes as they launched into motion.

They coasted to a stop in a clearing at the

bottom of the hill, Rose out of breath at the excitement of it all. She could hear the laughter of the others nearby, magnified by the cold wind, but it felt as if she was alone with Harry in the bower of winter trees. Frost hung from bare branches, sparkling like glass. It was quite magical, like a moment hovering out of time. She stared up at the diamond sparkle of it, dazzled.

'It's so beautiful, isn't it?' she whispered.

'Yes,' he answered, in a strangely hoarse voice.

Surprised, Rose glanced up to find he was staring not at the beauty around them, but at *her*. For an instant, all she could do was stare at him, captured by his gaze.

He gave her a rueful smile. 'When Charles and I were small, we had a nursemaid for a time who liked to read us fairy stories. One was about a winter queen, pale and shimmering in the snow. I haven't thought of it in years, until now.'

'Why now?'

'Because you look like her. A winter fairy queen in her ice palace. I had forgotten how beautiful it all could be.'

'Me? A fairy queen?' she whispered, amazed by such words. She knew she wasn't beautiful, that she was quite ordinary with her brown hair and her spectacles. Especially next to ladies such as her golden sister and her elegant cousin Jane. Yet she knew Harry was not a man to give compliments lightly, to say what he did not mean. He made her feel warm and glowing, all the way to her toes.

'Yes, with your pink cheeks and eyes glowing,' he said. 'And yet—' He broke off with a laugh, rubbing his hand over the back of his neck.

'Yet?' she whispered.

'Yet you, Rose, are real.' He suddenly took her gloved hand, holding it tightly in his. She curled her fingers around his, wondering at the feelings that came unbidden at his touch. 'Warm and real, not like an icy winter fairy at all. You have a—a kindness in you as warm as any fire.' He held her hand against his chest and through his thick wool coat she could feel the beat of his heart, flowing through her whole body.

'And so have you!' she cried, unable to hold back her words. 'A warmth, a kindness.'

He shook his head. 'Perhaps once. Long ago.'

Rose stared up at him, a bittersweet longing in her heart such as she had never known. She gave in to her feelings and leaned closer to him, letting her forehead rest on his shoulder. Suddenly she did not feel alone at all.

'What happened to it?' she said. 'What can bring it back?'

He was silent for a long moment, not looking at her but out into the distance, as if he was very far away from her at that moment. 'When I was in the army, I became friends with a young man from a small farm not far from here. He had a young wife and a child, and he would talk to me about them in the evenings when we were all near the fire. The way he spoke about them—I quite envied him!'

'Envied him?' she said.

'Yes. Such love, so much to look forward to when he returned to England—a real home. A place where he belonged.'

Had Harry not felt as if he had a place to belong? Rose reached out to touch his hand, wanting so much to reassure him, to tell him he *could* have that, could have all he dreamed of. But she couldn't find the right words. 'And has he gone home now?'

Harry shook his head. 'He was killed in battle. I saw him, through the smoke and the terrible noise, the screams. I tried to save him, but—it was much too late. I went to see his wife after I returned, before she went back to her own parents. She was so brave, so kind, trying to reassure *me* when I was the one who owed her everything.' He gave Rose that crooked half-smile that always made her heart ache. 'She rather reminded me of you.'

'Of me?' Rose said hoarsely.

'Yes. So kind, so brave. I have never forgotten her or her husband. Nor have I forgotten the terrors of battle. Not until now. Is this not a peaceful place?'

Rose swallowed hard past her threatening tears and nodded. 'Yes,' she said. 'With the snow and silence—it is most peaceful indeed.'

They were quiet for a long moment and somehow in that still, perfect hush Rose felt closer to him that she ever had to anyone.

'Shall we take another turn down the hill

before we have to leave?' he said finally. Rose nodded and in silence they made their way back up the hill. But it was not a heavy, uncomfortable silence. Indeed, Rose had not felt so utterly free of the chill of loneliness in a long time. And he still held her hand safely in his, leading her up the slippery slope.

At the top of the hill, she could see all the countryside around them, the fields laid out like an undulating blanket of grey and blue in the winter, the thicket of the woods, the sky stretching above them endlessly. 'How lovely it all is!' she exclaimed. 'At Aunt Sylvia's, I am indoors all the time. This is—is a wonderland!'

He smiled and it seemed brighter even than the light that broke through the clouds over their heads. 'We can even see Hilltop from here.'

'We can? Where?'

He pointed into the distance and Rose glimpsed a cluster of red brick and grey-stone chimneys in the distance. It looked like a castle in a fairy tale, just as he had said, with the last of the morning mist catching around its towers.

'It looks like something in your nurse-maid's stories,' she said. 'A magical castle.'

The corner of his lips quirked in a half-smile. 'Perhaps you would come to visit Hill-top one day?'

Rose felt her cheeks turn warm in the cold breeze and she looked away. What could he mean by such an invitation? She certainly knew better than to hope anything at all, but she couldn't help the little nervous flutter deep inside. 'I—of course. I would enjoy that very much.'

'We can make a party of it soon,' he said, his smile widening. 'Once I can make certain the house is presentable. Parts of it are very old, but I admit it does not look like a fairy tale close up.'

Rose nodded. If he intended for the others to come, surely he meant nothing by such an invitation. Jane was his neighbour, of course he would invite her house party there. 'Yes, of course.'

'Come along, you two!' she heard Jane call. She turned to see Jane and her husband at the foot of the hill, waving at them. Rose hoped they couldn't see her silly blush from there. 'We shall be late for the assembly to-night if we don't get back to Barton soon.'

'Shall we, then?' Harry said, holding out his hand to help her back on to the sled.

She laughed and took his hand in hers again. She had to enjoy every bit of that freedom while she had it. He sat down behind her, his strong, warm body blocking the cold wind, and they launched down the hill. It felt as if her heart would soar free with it and she laughed in sheer delight.

Rose peeked curiously out the carriage window as they made their way along the Barton village street towards the assembly rooms. In the daylight, the building was a perfectly ordinary long, low, brick structure meant for meetings and gatherings. For a holiday evening, though, it was quite transformed. Golden light spilled from every window and doorway, covering all with a warm sparkle in the dark winter night. Laughter rose and fell from the revellers making their way inside, blending with the strains of music as the small orchestra tuned their instruments to prepare for the dancing.

As soon as they rolled to a stop, Jane had taken Hayden's arm and disappeared into the crowd, leaving Emma and her husband and Rose to follow them. The rest of the party emerged from the next carriage, without Lady Fallon, who had been rather late and promised to come after. Harry and his brother were also coming after. Rose tried not to look for him, tried not to wonder if he would ask her to dance when he arrived. Their moment alone in the woods seemed so far away here in the noisy crowd.

After their wraps were left with the attendants, the Barton party joined the stream of merrymakers making their way up the stairs to the ballroom itself. It was a long, narrow chamber, the walls painted a pale blue to match the heavy curtains at the windows where the light drifts of snow could be seen, but everything was made warm for the season with garlands and wreaths of greenery. Tables draped in snowy linens held punch bowls and plates of sandwiches and cakes, interspersed with silver vases of holly.

As Emma and the others melted into the crowds, Rose accepted a glass of wonderfully warm negus and found a quiet corner where she could watch it all. Everyone wore their holiday best, silks and muslins and velvets, the young people smiling shyly at each other as they found dance partners, Jane and a few others making up card tables near the fireplaces at either end of the room. It was a lovely scene, like a painting or something in a song of holiday cheer. Rose only wished she had something to wear besides her grey silk, especially as she saw Lady Fallon at last make her entrance, very glamorous in midnight-blue velvet and black tulle.

Oh, well, Rose thought ruefully as she sipped at her drink. Her grey silk was perfectly respectable and no one had asked her to play for the dancing yet, as she usually did on the few occasions she was at a dance. It was a rather nice evening. She had certainly become good at holding up walls and that was where she got the best view.

She pressed as close as she could to the wall behind her, feeling the smoothness of the blue paper through the old silk of her gown and sipping at the rest of her drink as she took the measure of the crowd. Every party was different, unpredictable, even when it was the same people going about the same activities of dancing and cards and gossip.

It was a surprisingly large crowd, considering the damp, chilly night it was outside, with a few drifts of snow lazily floating down from the sky. She thought she wouldn't completely mind being home by a large fire with a good book herself, but she realised with a sudden wistful pang that she wished it was her own house, her own fire, a book of her choosing and maybe, if she was truly to dream big, someone to read it with. To laugh with.

An image popped into her mind of Harry smiling in the snow, laughing with her as their sled flew down the hill. Rose blinked hard, trying to push away such an enticing and impossible vision.

But—he *had* invited her to visit Hilltop, albeit with their rest of the party. It was surely a mere spur-of-the-moment politeness which meant no more than that. What if, by some wondrous chance, though, it was something a bit—more?

Rose shook her head at herself and gulped

down the last of her now cool drink. She had spent her whole life being the sensible one. She *had* to be, or her dear mother and sister would have been in even greater straits when her father died. Romantic dreams were luxuries. Luxuries she had always known couldn't be hers.

She glanced out the tall windows beyond the refreshment tables and saw that the snow was coming down a bit heavier, soft, sparkling flurries against the velvet night. Its wintry silence made the merriment indoors seem cosy and Rose couldn't help but wonder where Harry and his brother were. Surely they had not broken down on their journey to the village?

'Miss Parker,' she heard someone say and turned to see Emma Marton hurrying towards her, along with her husband and another lady, a tall, elegant woman in plain dark green velvet, who Rose recognised as Mrs Anson from their card game. 'Whatever are you doing here by yourself? And your glass is empty! David, dearest, could you fetch us some punch?'

David Marton, always such a kind and

obliging, not to mention ridiculously handsome man, smiled and gallantly kissed his wife's hand before he disappeared in the crowds around the refreshment tables.

Emma turned back to Rose and said, 'You have met Mrs Anson, yes, who manages my bookstore for me? Rose Parker is our own cousin and loves books quite as much as we do, I'm happy to say.'

'I'm very glad to see you again, Miss Parker,' Mrs Anson said with a smile. Rose was drawn to her at once and not just because she also wore spectacles. 'It's always marvellous to meet friends of Emma's, especially a fellow reader. Have you by chance tried the new Mrs Radcliffe? I found it quite chilling.'

'I haven't, though I must say I have been dying to have a peek at it,' Rose answered. 'I'm working as companion to an aunt, you see, and while she does enjoy reading aloud, her tastes do tend to run to sermons and not horrid novels. I must sneak off at bedtime to read by myself in the candlelight, which makes such tales even more fearsome.'

Mrs Anson laughed. 'I do sympathise. After I lost my husband, I too had to live with some aunts, until this position in Emma's wonderful shop came about. Now I can read to my heart's content.'

'And I could not keep the store without her,' Emma said. 'I think books have certainly saved our sanity, if not our very lives, at times, have they not?'

Rose laughed and nodded as David Marton came back with their drinks. The orchestra, a group of local musicians who Emma said were more noted for their volume than their ability to stay in tune, launched into the first dance and couples started to form into sets on the narrow, crowded dance floor. At the same moment, the door opened to admit a party of latecomers. Among them were Harry and his brother at last.

Harry did look so handsome in his dark blue evening coat and stark white cravat, Rose thought. In the candlelight, his scars could barely be seen and his smile was open and friendly, if a bit cautious. Rose glanced away, feeling her cheeks grow warm again, only to find herself being watched by Lady Fallon. The lady's head was tilted to one side, as if she was curious about something, a small frown on her lips. When she saw Rose looking at her, she gave a jaunty smile and turned away.

'Harry, Charles!' Emma called, waving them over. 'There you are at last. We were beginning to think something dreadful had happened to you.'

Harry laughed and Rose was struck by how it lit his whole face. Indeed, he seemed altogether brighter that evening. It was quite enchanting. 'Only an emergency in which Charlie could not choose his cravat.'

'The right cravat is an essential element of one's attire,' Charles said chidingly. 'It must suit the party atmosphere.'

Rose glanced at the cravat in question, but to her it looked as all such things did—white and starched into ruffled folds. Mrs Anson laughed and said, 'Oh, it does indeed. I see you have chosen an emerald pin as well, very suited to Christmas.'

Emma glanced between them, a thoughtful expression on her elfin face. 'Such a cravat does deserve a proper showing, Charles. Perhaps on the dance floor?'

'Of course,' Charles said with a bow. 'My

reeling skills are a bit rusty, but I would be honoured if you would be my partner, Lady Marton.'

Emma laughed and touched the small swell of her stomach under her velvet gown. 'Oh, no, I am not up to dancing tonight. I shall have to join my sister and the others for cards. But Mrs Anson does enjoy it so.'

Charles turned to Mrs Anson with a smile. 'Will you do me the honour, then, Mrs Anson? I promise not to tread on your slippers too much.'

Mrs Anson accepted with a smile and took Charles's arm to make her way into the set. Rose could feel Emma and Harry both looking at her and she fidgeted with her skirt to keep from blushing again.

'Shall we join them, Miss Parker?' Harry asked. She peeked up to find him smiling at her ruefully, as if he knew what she was thinking. 'My dancing skills have never been as fine as my brother's, but I'm sure we can learn together. It must be easier than guiding a sled.'

Rose laughed, put at her ease in an instant, as was always the case with him. 'It's been a long while for me as well, since Lily and I had girlhood lessons. I'm sure the dances we were taught then are most unfashionable by now, but perhaps if we just follow the others…'

'We danced well together before, did we not?' he said.

Rose smiled at the memory. 'Indeed we did.'

Harry offered her his arm and she slipped her gloved hand lightly on to his sleeve. His arm was warm and strong under her touch, reassuring as he led her through the crowd. She felt a strange, tingling sensation on the back of her neck, just under her heavy chignon of hair. Startled, she glanced back and found Lady Fallon watching her intently with narrowed eyes.

That look seemed—envious. Which was entirely ridiculous. Lady Fallon was a vivacious beauty, especially in her fashionable gown, ruby and diamond combs in her high-piled golden-red hair. Why would she look so at Rose, with her second-best, much-worn grey silk?

But then again—Rose did have Harry's

arm at the moment, she realised. She remembered much too well the first time they had met, when everyone said surely Captain St George would marry the lovely Helen. He'd left with his regiment and she married the rich Lord Fallon, but all of that was changed now.

Rose glanced up at Harry, uncertain, and he smiled back at her. The candlelight, the music and the laughter, the sweet-spicy cinnamon smell of Christmas and above all the feeling of Harry at her side—surely it was something, one small moment, she could savour? It couldn't last long, but it made her feel a wondrous holiday glow all the same.

She vowed to forget Lady Fallon, to forget Aunt Sylvia and her cold house, to forget everything else just for a moment. She did have to be so careful in her life. She was with Harry now for just one dance. His arm felt so strong, so steady under her touch. Surely such a man would hold her strong and steady, never letting her fall in the confusing twirls and reversals of a dance that was too much like life.

Maybe, just maybe, he would give her another of those smiles again, too.

* * *

Rose Parker was a most unusual young lady indeed. Harry had known that from the first moment they met, at that party so long ago, and now he was sure of it. She *did* remind him of that fairy queen in his story, but warm and real and laughing. It had been hard to part from her at the end of their dance, to lead Helen into the figures for the next set. Rose had been led away to play at the pianoforte and he couldn't see her any longer.

As a line of dancers separated him from Helen, Harry tried to catch a glimpse of Rose over the heads of the crowd packed close around them, but she had vanished. He could only see the top of her light brown hair. He almost laughed at himself for the pang of disappointment he felt.

There was no use for it. He was too old, too damaged, too burdened with responsibilities now to think about a young lady like Rose Parker. She was too pretty, too kind— and too caught in the traps of responsibility to family, just as he was. They would not be good for one another, not situated as they both were in life.

Yet that disappointment *was* there, and no mistaking it. When Rose was near, she always intrigued him. What was she thinking about, behind those unfathomable eyes? She was always watchful, always with that small smile curving on her shell-pink lips, as if she saw all around her and found it amusing, delightful, despite the straits she found herself in with her poor curate's wife of a sister and working as a companion for an elderly aunt. But none of it seemed to have affected her sweetness, her pleasure in the Christmas festivities.

He had no place for someone like Rose in his life now, not with Hilltop depending on him, and she had no room for him. Long ago, when he went into the army after a too-wild time as a young man, when he had caused much pain and trouble for his family, he had vowed he would change. He would fight for what was right, for his country and his home, and now he had to fulfil that vow. However he could.

'Harry, darling,' Helen said merrily. 'You must pay attention!'

He snapped back into the real world, the noisy, crowded assembly, and saw that Helen smiled at him as she held out her hands. It was their turn to twirl down the line and the others watched them impatiently.

Helen laughed and clasped his hand to spin and skip in the elaborate steps he somehow remembered from childhood classes, when he and Helen and Charlie had been schooled by a stern French dancing master with other loud children.

'You do remember how to be a gentleman,' she said as they turned in allemande.

'Just barely,' he answered. 'It must be your elegant influence.'

'Oh, I don't know. You did very well part-nering Miss Parker. I think you underesti-mate yourself, Harry,' she said. 'In so many ways.'

As she had underestimated him, leaving behind a possible future as a mere military wife to wed a lord? He almost asked her, but then he just laughed. All of that seemed so long ago. That Harry, and surely even that Helen, no longer existed. What did she want now?

What indeed did *he* want now? His life, a life that once was as regimented as a parade, was now like a grey cloud lowering over the horizon, obscuring all.

You need an heiress, he heard Charles say in his mind. And an heiress would indeed be an answer for Hilltop. He himself would admit that companionship, a partner, would be most welcome.

He looked down at Helen, at her brilliant smile, the flash of jewels in her hair, and for an instant he felt the tug of temptation towards a life that had never been his. A life of carefree glitter.

But then, over the swirl of the dancers, he glimpsed Rose Parker, laughing with the other musicians as her slender fingers lightly skipped over the keys. And he was drawn towards her soft warmth that was like a fire on a cold day, sustaining and sweet.

Rose deserved far more than what he had to offer, a wounded soldier whose house was falling down around him. That was one thing he did know for sure.

'Harry!' he heard Helen cry and suddenly realised he had once again lost the rhythm of the dance. Just like the reins of responsibility for Hilltop, he had to take them up again.

He took her hand and led her down the line again, Helen laughing as if it was all the greatest lark, as surely her life often was.

As they turned to circle the outside of the set, he glimpsed his brother standing on the sidelines, ignoring the elderly matron who chattered at his elbow. Charles grinned at Harry and raised his glass in salute.

Harry nodded back, but the delight in the party he had felt so briefly was gone.

'You see,' Jane said with a satisfied smile as she laid down her cards. Rather than dancing, she had decided another hand of whist with her husband and Emma and David was preferable, and now she was glad of it. From her seat at the table by the fire, she could observe the whole assembly. 'It is all coming off rather well.'

'What is?' Emma asked, frowning down at her hand of cards.

'My matchmaking, of course!' Jane said. 'I do like it when I have a fine idea.'

'Oh, my dear, no,' Hayden groaned. 'Surely you don't still think of that?'

'Think what?' Emma cried in confusion.

Her husband, who was accustomed to his in-laws' fancies, calmly laid down a card and smiled.

'Harry St George and Helen Fallon were once nearly betrothed, were they not?' Jane said. 'And now here they are, each of them single once again. And each has something the other needs. Why should they not fall for each other again?'

'Sometimes fate parts people for a good reason, Sister,' Emma said. 'Perhaps they were not meant for each other.'

'And sometimes two people must learn to find each other at the *right* time,' Jane said with a tender smile at her husband, whom she had once almost lost. 'It was just so with us.'

Hayden shook his head. 'But Captain St George and Lady Fallon are not us, my love.'

Jane glanced at the dance floor. 'They do look well together, though.'

'He looked well dancing with Rose Parker, too,' Emma said with a sneaking smile.

'Rose Parker?' Jane said in surprise.

'Yes. And surely their personalities are rather well suited,' Emma said. 'They are both so quiet, so easy to be around.'

Jane looked at Rose, who sat at the pianoforte. She had not thought of such a thing, but Emma did have a point. And a lady without a fortune did need a home, one better than with an old aunt.

'No,' she murmured. 'Harry must surely consider Hilltop now and all its tenants. And we must find someone well settled for Rose.'

Emma looked doubtful, but she nodded. 'Just as you say, Jane.'

And while they were so occupied with romance, David won the hand easily.

Chapter Ten

Charles St George took a deep drag on his cheroot, tasting the cherry-smoke darkness at the back of his throat, before he exhaled the silvery plume into the frosty air of the small garden behind the assembly rooms. He could hear the music from the windows behind him, the stomp of dancing feet, the beat of the music, but it seemed very far away, like something in a dream.

It had been much the same on the Continent. The music and laughter in casinos and ballrooms, the subtle dance of glances and smiles, the silent language everyone seemed to understand but him. At least at first. Eventually he learned it, even mastered it. But here, back at the home he had shunned for so long—it all seemed strange again. A cacophony he couldn't quite make out clearly. All those happy couples in their contented homes—Jane and Hayden, Emma and David, and all their friends and their children. How did they do it? Charles found it such a mystery.

He thought of the people, especially the women, he had known in Europe. The beautiful, sophisticated ladies with their satins and their jewels, their brittle laughter. *That* was what he knew. Lightness, flirtations, fleeting moments. Songs and laughter around the Christmas candles he could not fathom. And yet...

Yet he longed for it, wanted it with a primitive fierceness he hadn't felt since he was a child and so wanted to belong. Yet he never had, except for his brother.

Charles inhaled from his cheroot again and stared up into the sky. It was a cold night, so crisp the breeze felt it could snap in two, but the sky was clear now, the earlier snow ceased. The stars sparkled like diamonds on a lady's black velvet gown, glittering so he wanted to reach out and feel their heat on his skin. Feel alive again.

Once, he would have longed to paint the scene, the bare trees against the candlelit windows, the elusive sparkle of the stars. Once his paintbrush could make sense of so many things around him, but now even that urge had deserted him. After what had happened to Harry on the battlefield, seeing Hilltop in such trouble, painting seemed frivolous.

Surely his father had been right. Art was useless for a man. Charles gave a bitter laugh and raised his cheroot to his lips again.

'Do you happen to have one of those to spare?' he heard a soft voice ask.

Surprised, he spun around to find Helen standing behind him. With the sparkle of jewels in her hair, the soft shimmer of her blue gown, she looked like a goddess. But silk gloves and tulle sleeves were no use in the cold wind and she shivered a bit in spite of her bright smile.

She had always been beautiful and so far above his touch. But now there was a lack of a smile in her eyes, a disillusionment like his own.

'Of course,' he replied quickly, not knowing what to say to her, how to reach her. All his skills of flirtation learned in those spa towns seemed useless with Helen. As if they would bounce right off that diamond-hard, brilliant shell that had grown around her beautiful self since he had seen her last. She no longer seemed to be the girl he had known for so long, the beautiful, fiery, adventurous Helen, the one who made him envy Harry for being her intended.

But that was a very long time ago. None of them were the same people now.

He took out his silver cheroot case and offered her one, lighting it from the remains of his own. Then he removed his velvet evening coat and tucked it around her shoulders against the cold night.

She smiled up at him and it seemed a different smile than before, softer, more tentative. More like the Helen he once knew and he felt a flash of something strangely like hope.

'It's a vile habit, I know,' she said, balancing the thin cigar between her gloved fingers. 'You must not tell anyone.'

Charles laughed. 'Your secret is always safe with me.'

Helen laughed, too, and it sounded like music on the cold breeze. 'You are clever to find such a hiding place, Charlie. Sometimes it feels as if there isn't one place left to disappear in all the world.'

'I'm surprised you would ever want to disappear. Are you not the belle of every ball?'

She smiled, her oval face wreathed in smoke. 'How can I live with such a thing all the time? It's amusing sometimes, of course. But never to get away from everyone watching...' She broke off and shook her head. 'One has to always, always smile, or the rumours will fly.'

That sounded intriguing. 'What sort of rumours?'

'Oh, you know, Charlie. I am sure that you, of all people, know.' Her smile turned bitter again.

'Helen,' he said carefully. 'What was it really like, being married to Fallon?'

Helen took a deep inhale of the smoke, not looking at him. 'Oh, you know. It is an old title that opens every door. Is that not what every girl wants? A title, a place in society, a role as a leader of fashion.'

Charles nodded. A marriage to Harry could not have given her that, it was true. 'Was it what *you* wanted?'

She shrugged. 'Of course. What else is there? To be a woman like Miss Parker, forced to be a companion or a governess?' She glanced at the party behind the windows, an unreadable expression on her face. 'But she is kind, isn't she?'

'Who?' Charles asked, unable to follow the meander of Helen's thoughts.

'Miss Parker, of course. She is sweet. Pretty, in her quiet way. She makes people around her want to smile, to feel that the world *can* be good, just as she is. She has such power, but she doesn't know it. Nice people like her never do.' She studied the stars high above their heads for a moment. 'Sometimes I wish I could be like that. Could deserve—more.'

Charles felt his heart ache at her sadness and he longed to take it away, to erase it as if it had never been, even as he knew he was not the person for such a task. He had too many ugly burdens of his own, hidden inside. 'Helen,' he said roughly. It took all the self-control he had left not to add the word *darling*, not to take her into his arms and hold her close against the cold world that seemed to hold them both prisoners. 'You deserve so very much. You deserve *everything*.'

She turned to look at him, her pale, perfect face filled with surprise. Her eyes were wide, startled. But she quickly covered it with that hard, brilliant smile. 'Charlie, you *are* a dear. But you don't know what I've done in my life.'

'Nor do you know what I have done, what I have seen. You can tell me anything you want, Helen, anything at all and I won't be shocked.'

'No, I don't think you would.' She glanced in the windows behind them, watching the shadows of the dancers pass beyond the glass. 'But what of Harry? What do you think he would think?'

Was that it, then? Helen still wanted Harry after all this time? Charles felt something he had not in a long time—sadness. 'He is your friend, too.'

She gave a bright little laugh. 'Oh, yes. My friend. Harry is so good, so like Miss Parker in some ways, isn't he? He has always put others before himself. His country, his duty. Once I thought that so boring. Didn't you, Charlie dear?'

'Maybe I did, once.'

'But we are all older now. Isn't that supposed to make us see so much clearer?' She turned away from the dancers and smiled up at him, a beacon of pure, bright light in the dark night. 'Tell me, do you still paint?'

'No. The will to see clear enough to put something down on canvas seems to have deserted me.'

Helen tilted her head as she studied him. 'I am indeed sorry to hear that. I loved your paintings. You made the world look so beautiful, like a place where one could be at peace. Do you remember a scene you did once of your mother's rose garden?'

He nodded, his thoughts going back to the summer beauty of the garden, the scent of the roses on the warm breeze—and Helen walking along the paths, a solitary figure in white he tried to capture. 'Yes.'

'It was wondrous. Like heaven should be, I think. I have never found a place to equal it. Nor, I suppose, have you.'

He shook his head. Her smile faded and she turned away to crush the end of her cheroot under her satin shoe. She slid off his coat and held it out to him.

'Thank you, Charlie,' she said simply and then she was gone, hurrying back into the crowded assembly and leaving only a trace of her exotic jasmine perfume behind.

Find an heiress for Hilltop, Charles had told Harry so blithely. So foolishly, as if heiresses were mere pieces to be moved around a chessboard. Surely their old friend Helen would do. How he regretted those words now. Helen was no mere heiress, no mere solution to a problem or childhood memory. She was so much more, had become so much more. And she deserved a fine man like Harry to make her truly smile again.

Charles look up at the cold, hard stars and found that they seemed even further away than ever before. Just like Helen herself.

Chapter Eleven

Harry stood back and studied the façade of the house with a careful, critical eye. Hilltop was not as modern or comfortable as Barton, he had to admit that. It had retained the look of an earlier time, with its rough stone walls and old towers, its wavy, thick-glass windows gazing out at the world, but letting little of it in.

But he liked the look of it and he hoped Rose would, too. She seemed to enjoy old tales, stories of fairy-tale castles. Hilltop did have just such an appearance.

Why did he care so much about whether or not Rose liked his house?

He picked up the holly wreath that lay at his feet and hung it on the old, stained, stout wooden door. It gleamed there, all glossy green leaves and bright red berries, brightening the grey stone and sending out a welcome on the cold day. It made him think of Rose herself, so warm in a cold world.

The day of the planned visit to Hilltop dawned bright and clear, cold but with a rare turquoise sky arching overhead. Rose was mesmerised by its beauty, by the prospect of the lovely day ahead, the rare treat of a ride, the chance to see Harry in his own home. She wanted to enjoy it to the fullest and not think too hard about what her feelings meant, what hurt they might bring her in the future.

Harry had ridden ahead and only Jane and Hayden elected to come along on the excursion. All the others wanted to stay near the fireplace with their cards and newspapers. Jane and her husband lagged behind Rose on the short ride, whispering and laughing together, like a pair of newly wed lovebirds free of their children and duties for a few hours.

Rose, too, felt a rare sense of freedom, of lightness. It was something she barely even remembered feeling before. She hadn't been able to ride in a long time, and at first she felt quite uncertain in the saddle, even though Jane assured her this was the gentlest mare in the Barton stable. But it had all come back to her in a wonderful rush, the power of the reins in her hands, the freedom of speed. The deliciousness of forgetting everything else for a moment.

It was so much like dancing with Harry, that feeling that her feet could leave the ground and she could fly free.

She urged her horse into a gallop along the pathway, winding their way up a hill beyond the Barton woods. She laughed as the cold wind caught at her hat and rushed over her cheeks. Yes—it was indeed like dancing, but only dancing with Harry!

She reined in her horse at the crest of the hill to wait for Jane and Hayden. From that vantage point, high above the pale rolling fields, she could see for what seemed like miles and miles. Barton Park, with all its fine, noisy company, and even her calmly dutiful life with Aunt Sylvia, were left far behind, and there was only that endless sky above her.

She remembered how she had felt once,

so long ago, when she had been impossibly young and the world full of all the opportunities she had read about in books. It hadn't turned out that way at all, of course. But here, now, at Christmas, she did recall how it felt to be that girl.

Her horse pawed restlessly at the frosty ground as Rose twisted around in the saddle to look towards where she knew the chimneys of Hilltop lay. She didn't know what she expected to see beyond the greystone walls that bisected Barton, Hilltop and Emma's home at Rose Hill. Perhaps a different land, a fairy land of clouds and mysterious groves, like in the story Harry had said his nursemaid once read to him.

Yet it all looked much the same, fallow winter fields, hills and half-frozen streams, all laid out like a patchwork blanket sewn together with those stone walls and fringed around the outside with woods.

In the distance, though, she glimpsed old brick chimneys and towers, and a curl of smoke that seemed to beckon a welcome. The house at Hilltop, just as Harry had pointed it out to her on their sled ride.

She glanced back over her shoulder to see that Jane and Hayden still lagged behind, making slow progress up the hillside. They waved at her, laughing as if they too felt the precious, fragile power of the day, and she waved back.

She urged the horse forward, down the slope of the hill and on to a wider path, lined on either side with railed fences. Down there, in the shelter of a small valley, the light seemed greyer, more shadowed. Over the fields stood a clutch of cottages, the white-washed and thatched houses of Hilltop tenants. When she turned through an open set of gates, once finely wrought iron in a pattern of pineapples and pomegranates but now rusted, she found Hilltop itself.

She remembered the fanciful thoughts of fairy tales and almost could have vowed she had truly found herself inside one. Unlike Barton, which had been renovated and re-decorated over many years, Hilltop looked like something from a medieval world. It was built of old grey stone, overgrown with yellowing ivy, round crenelated towers still guarding its four corners, with mullioned windows staring down at her like ancient eyes. She wouldn't have been surprised to see a moat and a drawbridge, with knights galloping over it and swords drawn.

As if to prove she had entered a medieval dream, she heard the pounding of hooves behind her, like those knights. She glanced back to see that it was only Jane and Hayden, catching up with her. They were laughing, as if they had been in a merry race, and it brought her back to the present day, to the reality of where and who she was. Just plain Rose Parker, lady's companion with cloudy dreams of romance.

She turned back to the house, suddenly nervous to see Harry again.

'It is a tiny bit gloomy, is it not?' Jane said, studying the great, thick, nail-studded fortress of the front door. 'But then again, so was Barton once. It only takes a bit of style to bring it into the comfortable modern day.'

Hayden laughed. 'Only when the style has your impeccable taste, my love.'

'Nothing so easy, as you well know,' Jane said. 'What do you think, Rose?'

Rose looked up at the towers, so much like

some place a fairy queen would really live in, magical and ancient. 'I think it looks enchanting. Like Sleeping Beauty's palace.'

'How right you are!' Jane exclaimed. 'One kiss and all would be well again.'

The doors opened with a great, rusty squeal and Harry appeared at the top of the cracked stone steps. In his tweeds and doeskin breeches, he looked like the country squire he was, not the solider he used to be. Rose found she liked both personas equally.

He had that wry half-smile he wore so often, but the bright gleam in his eye gave her hope he was indeed happy to see her there at Hilltop. Just as *she* was happy to be there, to see him and his home again.

'So you found your way here at last,' he called, making his way down the steps.

'Oh, you must blame our tardiness entirely on me, Harry!' Jane said merrily as she and Hayden entered the courtyard. 'It is too lovely a day to be inside, but we are so excited to see Hilltop again. You and Charlie have become much too reclusive.'

'I fear the old place is in no shape for fine parties,' Harry said. 'But I hope old friends can start to darken this warped old door again. The housekeeper is beside herself with excitement and has laid on a splendid tea.'

'I'm happy to hear that, for I am quite famished,' Rose said. 'I don't know how you fine military men ride for weeks! I've only been in the saddle for an hour and am thoroughly exhausted.'

'We can't have that, now, can we?' Harry reached up to help her down from her horse.

They stood there for a long moment, his hands warm at her waist, their bodies mere inches from each other. Rose couldn't seem to stop herself from leaning into him and inhaled deeply of his scent, cool wind and citrus soap lingering on his coat. How wonderful it felt to be so close to him again, like a delightful, delicious forbidden treat. She had a fierce longing to throw her arms about his neck and hold on to him, to let that lovely new feeling wash over her and carry her away. She felt his shoulders stiffen under her touch, as if he could read her thoughts.

She stepped back reluctantly, feeling a sharp pang at losing his closeness. She knew she had to enjoy such feelings in the moment, to store them up for memories in the lonely future. She turned to study the house before her.

Close up, she saw it was not quite the fairy tale she had first taken it for, though the sense of being a dwelling slumbering under a spell was still quite strong. The tiles of the roof were cracked and chipped, even broken away in places, shattered on the old cobblestones of the courtyard. Some of the windows of the upper floor were boarded up and the flower-beds that had once lined the drive in colour-ful profusion were overgrown.

Yet there was a wreath of holly and ev-ergreen hung over the door, a brave note of bright colour. 'You have a holly wreath!' she said. 'When Lily and I were children, our fa-ther always said we must have holly at our door for Christmas. He said the holiday spir-its would hide under the leaves to stay out of the winter cold and they would leave a bless-ing in return.'

Harry's smile widened. 'And did it work?'

Rose laughed. 'I don't know. Lily and I would stay up all hours of the night trying to glimpse them, but we never did. Though on Christmas morning, next to our breakfast plates, there were always extra sweets from the fairies.' She paused for a moment and in her mind she saw Lily small again, their mother's secret smiles with their father, the magical expectation of the day. 'It is strange. I haven't thought of that in so long.'

'I admit I had no thought of spirits when I had it put up there. I merely wanted you to see something pretty at Hilltop. I fear you'll be disappointed by the lack of festive decorations inside, though.' He led her up the old stone steps and swung open the doors, and Jane and Hayden trailed behind them, arm in arm. 'Most of the few servants we have left here have gone back to their families until Boxing Day and it's rather bare and cold.'

Rose had to laugh. 'You should see Aunt Sylvia's home. It is bare and cold every day, not to mention deathly quiet. This is…' She caught her breath at the sudden sight of the great hall she found herself in. 'Not dull at all. It's like something from King Arthur.'

She spun around in a circle, taking it all in. Just like the exterior of the house, the interior looked just as a fairy tale should. The great hall soared upwards, bisected by a wide stone staircase lined with an ornate iron balustrade that had fallen away in places. A huge iron chandelier hung high overhead, meant to illuminate the ancient, shredded pennants on the wall, the shields and swords hanging on the peeling walls, speaking of ancient times of St George glory.

'How very unfashionable, Harry,' Jane said with a laugh, removing her riding hat and gloves. Rose pulled her thoughts away from the Camelot fascination and followed suit. They left their accessories on the one piece of furniture, an old mosaic table, and Harry took their cloaks.

Rose fidgeted with her skirt, wishing she had a more à la mode habit, not just her old green wool one. It felt so out of place in the grandeur.

'Not much to be done about the fashion now, I'm afraid,' Harry said, a rueful smile in his tone. 'But I won't force you to take your tea in this great, chilly room.'

He led them along a long, narrow corridor, past a series of closed doors. Where one or two were open a crack, Rose glimpsed chambers shrouded with canvas covers, windows covered with dusty, faded velvet curtains, bare spots on the walls where paintings had once hung, empty cabinets whose *objets* had once been displayed.

Rose remembered the rumours that Harry needed a rich wife for his estate, for his duties, and she wondered sadly if that was all too correct.

Harry led them into a small sitting room at the end of the hallway and it was like stepping into another house altogether. The wallpaper, though much faded, was a lovely yolk-yellow with matching curtains at the windows and yellow and white striped upholstery on the chairs drawn close to a blazing fire in the white marble grate. A woman's portrait hung over the carved mantel, a lady with Charles St George's curling hair and Harry's eye colour, clad in yellow silk and pearls, smiling out at the world with her hands elegantly folded in her lap. A table was laid out with a tarnished silver teapot and china painted with small purple flowers, plates of sandwiches and iced cakes.

'Is that your mother?' Rose asked. 'How elegant she was.'

'Yes. This was her favourite room. Thankfully my father never touched it, or we wouldn't have a comfortable place to sit,' Harry answered, smiling at the painting. 'Please, everyone, do make yourselves comfortable.'

Rose perched on the edge of one of the chairs, unable to be rid of the feeling that Mrs St George was watching them, judging to see if they were worthy to be in her sitting room, in her home.

'Shall I pour?' Jane asked, reaching for the teapot. 'I fear I don't remember much about your mother, Harry, but my parents always said she used to give such lovely parties here. She was obviously a lady of fine taste.'

'Indeed she was,' Harry answered. 'Hilltop hasn't been the same since we lost her.'

Jane passed around the cups. 'They did say Hilltop was once quite the social centre of the neighbourhood! My mother said artists, politicians and leaders of fashion of all sorts came here. It must have been extraordinary.'

'Yes,' Harry said. 'Everyone loved my mother. My father could not do without her.'

'Such a sad and romantic tale,' Jane said. 'But Hilltop still has such potential. It could be that way again!'

'I fear I don't have such a social disposition, my dear Jane,' Harry said. He laughed, but Rose could sense something lurking just beneath, a tension, a discomfort. She wanted to soothe it, to tell him his home would be again as it was with his mother, but she didn't know how. Except for that wealthy heiress. She couldn't be that. Only the beautiful Helen Fallon could.

'Oh, Harry, no one expects the man to make a house a real home,' Jane said. 'That is the wife's job. I am sure your mother would agree.' She nodded towards the smiling, beautiful woman in the portrait.

'I am sure she would,' Harry said. 'But you must talk to Charlie about such matters, he is far more handsome and cosmopolitan than me. No fine lady would look twice at a battle-scarred old man like myself. Would you care for a sandwich?'

He passed around the plates of delicacies

and the talk turned to lighter matters, Jane's plans for a Christmas ball, the cold weather. The hour passed most pleasantly and, as the fire died down, Harry knelt down to build it up again.

'Oh, Harry, surely that is not your job,' Jane said with a laugh.

Harry tossed her a grin over his shoulder as he bent over the hearth stones, a wonderful, lighthearted smile Rose wanted to see again. 'I did learn one or two things in the army. I can't let my skills go rusty now.'

Rose sat back and watched as he rebuilt the fire in the grate and he soon had it roaring high enough to warm three rooms. The long, lean muscles of his back and broad shoulders shifted and flexed against his fine tweed coat and she remembered how those shoulders felt under her touch as they danced. The heat and strength of him, the way he made her feel so safe.

And she was not the only one he kept safe. He spent his life doing just that, looking after others, in the army and now at his family home. She knew he would never turn away from that duty.

She remembered his story of the young farmer he knew in the army, the one who had died and left his family behind, and Harry's longing for home, his need to do the right thing by his people. She knew those things would never change about him.

'Would you like to see more of the house?' he asked.

'Oh, yes!' Jane answered eagerly. 'I remember it in your mother's time, it was so lovely.'

'I'm afraid I don't have my mother's fine taste,' Harry said. 'But maybe you and Miss Parker could offer some female advice?'

Jane laughed, and took her husband's arm. 'Lead on, Harry!'

He took them through a series of rooms, most of them sparsely furnished or with canvas covers over chairs and tables, but it was still an intriguing house indeed, with old linenfold panelling on the walls, doors that led on to mysterious passages, vaulted ceilings with fading paintings of knights and ladies.

Jane and Hayden drifted away into another room, their voices echoing back to them, but

Rose was enchanted by the paintings high above her head.

'How lovely they are,' she murmured.

'My mother commissioned an artist to make them when she first moved here,' he said. 'They are rather faded now, but I think they suit the house. The fair maidens and the castles…'

'It's so enchanting,' she said, spinning towards him. 'Just like—like you, Harry.'

He took her hand and spun her in a dancing circle. 'It suits *you*, Rose.' Something in his hoarse voice caught her, held her, and she looked up at him in a haze.

He turned his face to kiss the inside of her wrist, the pulse that beat there so frantically at the nearness of him. His breath was so warm and vital and delicious on her bare skin, a fantasy she could hardly have dared dream could come true. If only she could do the same for him, could make *him* feel safe. Help him.

But she was poor and he had to protect his home now. She couldn't do all she wanted for him.

'I—we should find Jane,' she said and broke

away from him to hurry away. She felt so foolish, running away like that, but she didn't know what else to do. She needed to be near other people, to find shelter in the decorum of a group.

But she found there wouldn't be much 'decorum', for Jane and Hayden were kissing in the pale sunlight that drifted from the windows of the drawing room. They broke apart guiltily, and Rose had to laugh at the blush on her cousin's cheeks, as if they were naughty newlyweds.

Harry came up behind her and he laughed, too, putting her at ease once more. She would have to forsake his company soon enough. Surely she could enjoy that one afternoon with him?

'It looks like the sun is out now,' Harry said. 'We should take advantage of it. I was just going to ask Miss Parker if she would like to ride out with me to meet some of my tenants.'

'To visit your tenants? Really?' Rose said in surprise, feeling suddenly shy after what had happened upstairs. What might they think of her?

'I can hardly leave you to wander alone on my estate, especially you, Jane,' he said. 'I remember what a troublemaker you were in our youth.'

'Me?' Jane cried. 'Such calumny. It was always Emma and Charlie climbing trees and scaring the grouse. Hayden, you should call him out!'

Hayden laughed. 'I can't duel with a man for telling the truth, my love.'

Jane sighed. 'I suppose not. And we *are* fortunate to have such lovely, quiet neighbours. Very well, Harry, you may live.'

Harry laughed. 'Thank you, Jane.'

'I wouldn't mind calling on some tenants of my own,' Jane said. 'Rose, why don't you go with Harry and we shall meet back at Barton?'

'Are you sure?' Rose asked in surprise. Alone, with Harry? It sounded quite thrilling.

'Of course. Someone must add a kind, tender touch for Harry's poor tenants. He must scare them to pieces with his military ways,' Jane said.

'I will take care of her,' Harry said. And she was quite sure he would.

* * *

'Jane, my darling,' Hayden said. 'What are you thinking now?'

Jane gave him an innocent smile and he quirked a dark brow. She feared she could seldom fool him after all the years of their marriage, all they had been through. 'I am merely thinking we really should call on the Porters while we are so near, since Mrs P. has the new baby. And Harry *is* quite likely to frighten someone, he does glower so since he came home.' But then again, she thought, he had not really glowered much in the last couple of days and not at all on this day.

'But that is not all you are thinking. I know you were thinking of matchmaking for poor Harry before this party began.'

'Perhaps I was,' Jane admitted. 'I just can't help it, darling. I do want all our friends to be as happy as we are.'

'And your kind heart is why I love you so much. You never give up on anyone, even on me. Harry St George is a good man and has certainly been through a great deal, war and wounds, his father dying so suddenly, the responsibilities of a place like Hilltop. More than any man should have to at once. But you and I both know a lady like Miss Parker can't help him now.'

Jane frowned. 'Rose is a lovely girl, even though she doesn't realise it.'

'She is lovely. And kind, calm and sensible. She rather reminds me of someone.'

'Really?' Jane said with a pang of jealousy. 'Who?'

Hayden laughed. 'You, of course.'

'Then why should I not try to help them along? I know I did think of him and Lady Fallon at first, but...'

'There is just one flaw in your plan, my dear, and I fear it's a large one.'

'What is that?'

'Miss Parker has no money. And Hilltop is falling down.'

'Oh. Yes.' Jane sighed, wishing she had a different, more romantic argument to make, but she couldn't find one. She glanced back at the crumbling chimneys of Hilltop and frowned. Harry St George was indeed a man who took his responsibilities seriously and his old family home was a large responsibility indeed. She knew that all too well, remembering the days when her beloved Barton was also crumbling. 'Perhaps Lady Fallon will have to be it, then.'

Still—most problems *did* have a solution, Jane told herself, if one could only think hard enough.

Rose followed Harry down the slope of a hill and along a path, narrow enough only for their horses to walk single file. Beyond the thicket of trees and out of sight of the main house, a row of cottages was laid out, near to the fields, but not as far out as the larger farms. Unlike the main house, they looked snug and tidy and recently repaired, their walls freshly whitewashed. She could hear laughter through the new windows and the timbered doors were decorated with greenery wreaths.

Harry led her past more cottages, including one that seemed to be a small shop with holiday sweets decorating the front bow window. Just beyond, in a thicket of tall trees, was a brick building. Unlike the cottages, it had no windows and the splintered door hung loose on its hinges.

'The school,' Harry said simply, solemnly, as he gestured at the building. 'My mother had it built for the tenants' children, but after she died my father closed it and it fell into disrepair.'

'Did it have many pupils?'

'A fair number. My mother thought the estate children should know reading, writing and sums, things to help them run prosperous farms and homes later.'

'She was quite right,' Rose answered, thinking of her own youthful lessons of sewing and dancing, and how little use they were. 'What of trades, such as sewing and cooking for the girls? Perhaps even training as ladies' maids or milliners?'

'That is a fine idea indeed,' Harry said, smiling as he examined the old building. 'I should very much like to repair this place and re-open the school. But such things can be—well…'

'Expensive. Yes,' Rose said ruefully. She glanced back at the half-hidden cottages, with their snug roofs and walls. 'Yet you have done so much just in the short time since you returned. The tenants' homes look so well tended. And the fields look as if they can be good producers in the summer. Jane says the soil is fine in this area. The price of corn has gone up since the end of the war and the weather this winter has been mild enough until this week.'

He gave her a surprised-looking smile. 'You're very well informed.'

Rose laughed. 'I know. Most unladylike. But part of my job is to read to Aunt Sylvia. She mostly prefers sermons and a few novels, but she does take many of the newspapers and I like to glance at them when I have the chance. Hilltop could do very well, I think, with just a bit of care.'

'Which is what I hope to give.' He gestured with his riding crop down a wider lane. 'The Perkins's farm is just this way, follow me.'

He led her down a path lined with thick hedges to a two-storey farmhouse, also whitewashed and with a thatched roof, but the paint was fresh and the thatch new, with a neat little vegetable garden enclosed by a low fence. Chickens peeked around the doorstep and the door was painted a dark green and hung with a holly wreath. Rose could feel someone watching them from the windows, studying them, *her*—the woman with Hilltop's master. Surely they were curious. Rose just wished she could be more than a visitor.

'I—perhaps I should wait for you here,' she said.

'It's much too cold for that, Rose! Besides, I assure you the Perkins family are the kindest of people. Their family has been at Hilltop for years and I know how much they love company.'

'I...' But she could make no more protests, as the door swung open. A man stood there, tall with a farmer's broad shoulders, a little girl with long, blond braids holding his hand. The man smiled and waved, and the girl practically jumped up and down in excitement. The warmth of their greeting seemed to spill right out of the cottage and wrapped around Rose like the lantern light and the scent of fresh-baked bread.

'Captain St George!' the man said. 'We didn't expect to see you here on such a cold day.'

'I got your message about the roof,' Harry

said as he swung down from his saddle. He reached up to help Rose and she again seized the moment of his touch and stored it up in her memory. 'And I heard your mother was ailing. I hope she has recovered.'

'Aye, thanks to the doctor you sent to see her last week. She's doing better than she has in an age.'

'You send a doctor to your tenants?' Rose whispered to Harry, though she was not surprised at all. Being the most dutiful landlord seemed entirely like him.

'Of course. Since I've returned, it's my job. Not that there is much any doctor can do for old Mrs Perkins, I fear. She is usually much too feisty to follow his advice.'

Rose laughed, thinking of Aunt Sylvia and all the fine London physicians she had thrown out on their ears. 'I know the sort very well.'

'Captain, Captain!' the little girl cried and came skipping down the garden pathway to tug at Harry's coat-tails. 'I'm getting a new doll for Christmas.'

Harry laughed and swung the child up into his arms, twirling her around until she shrieked with giggles. 'Are you indeed, Peggy? A fine gift for a fine girl!'

'But Papa doesn't know I know, so it's a secret.' She peeked curiously over his shoulder at Rose. 'Who is this?'

Harry gave her another twirl, and Rose laughed along with her, enchanted by this glimpse of a light-hearted Harry. He so rarely made an appearance. 'This is Miss Rose Parker, a guest at Barton Park,' he said. 'Miss Parker, this is Miss Peggy Perkins.'

Rose gave a little curtsy. 'How do you do, Miss Perkins? I am very pleased to meet you.'

Peggy studied her closely. 'You're very pretty.'

'Indeed she is,' Harry said, smiling at Rose over Peggy's head.

Rose felt her cheeks turning warm again and looked away with a nervous laugh.

'Peggy, stop chattering to the Captain and let him come inside where it's warm,' her father called.

Harry set Peggy on her feet and she led them through the doorway. 'Oscar Perkins, this is Miss Parker, one of the guests at Barton for the holiday.'

Mr Perkins didn't seem at all surprised his landlord would bring a strange lady into his house at Christmas, or if he was his wide smile didn't show it. He gave her a bow. 'You're most welcome, Miss Parker, as would be any friend of the Captain. I only wish we had a grander reception to offer you!'

Rose glanced around at the neatly swept stone floor, the dried bundles of herbs hung from the smoke-darkened rafters that perfumed the air with lavender and rosemary, the whitewashed walls. It all reminded her of her mother's cosy cottage, the cottage that meant Rose had to work for Aunt Sylvia to make sure it was affordable.

She felt suddenly a bit sad and wistful, and silly for forgetting the real world outside even for a moment.

'Your home is lovely, Mr Perkins,' she said. 'And so kind of you to receive me so close to Christmas. You must be busy.'

'Offer the lady some tea, Oscar!' a querulous old voice called from beyond an open door. 'Show the manners I taught you.'

Mr Perkins flushed. 'My mother. She does like to, er, express herself.'

Rose laughed, again thinking old Mrs Perkins must be a lot like Aunt Sylvia. 'Some tea would be most welcome.'

'There are cakes, too,' little Peggy said. 'I helped to make them.'

'Then they must be delicious,' Rose answered. She studied the bright-eyed girl and remembered the abandoned school. How much good such a place could do for girls like Peggy! If teachers and books could be paid for and the building repaired.

'Peggy, why don't you take Miss Parker to see your grandmother while I show the Captain the roof?' Mr Perkins said.

Peggy took Rose's hand to lead her towards the open door. Rose glanced back to see Harry talking to his tenant in a low, serious voice, the two of them nodding. The light-hearted man who had swung Peggy into the air was gone again.

The sitting room was a most cosy space, small but comfortable with well-worn, shabby furnishings brightened with pretty yellow cushions and the walls painted a summery blue. A tiny, grey-haired lady sat by the fire wrapped in shawls, a white cap perched on her head. Mrs Perkins did indeed look much like a less fancy version of Aunt Sylvia, right down to her bright blue, all-seeing eyes. Rose hovered uncertainly in the doorway.

'Granny, Captain St George brought a lady to visit us,' Peggy announced. 'Her name is Miss Parker.'

'A lady?' the elder Mrs Perkins said, those perceptive eyes sweeping over Rose, taking in her plain hat and outdated riding habit. 'It's about time he did that. Past time he got himself engaged. Hilltop has been too long without a proper mistress.'

Rose laughed nervously. 'I fear I am only a guest at Barton Park, Mrs Perkins. I teach music to the Fitzwalters' children.'

'Oh. Well. That is a disappointment. But I suppose you had better sit down, anyway. Peggy, dear, go fetch the tea, will you?'

As Peggy hurried away on her errand, Rose sat down on the stool next to Mrs Perkins's armchair. The fire was warm after the chilly day and the cottage pleasantly cosy.

'Perhaps you could persuade Lady Ramsay to find the Captain a suitable bride, then,' Mrs Perkins suggested. 'One who could make all the improvements this place needs.'

'Perhaps she could,' Rose said. 'And I would be most interested to hear what improvements you would suggest, Mrs Perkins, if the right Mrs St George could be found.'

Mrs Perkins smiled. 'I could make a long list, Miss Parker, indeed I could. The school needs to be re-opened, the fallow fields put into production again. Once, long ago, when I was a girl, the Captain's grandfather ran the estate and a fine landlord he was. Always concerned, always taking care of any problem right away. But his son...'

'The Captain's father?'

'Bah.' The old lady scowled. 'He didn't have a thought for anything but himself. Locked himself up in that house when his wife died, leaving us on our own. Running off his own sons. Master Charles—now there is a bonny young man, but I fear he takes too much after his father.'

'And does the Captain take after him?'

'Never! The Captain is a good man, a dutiful one. Look what he sacrificed in battle. Wounded like that and then coming home to a shambles. 'Tis a great shame. But we know he will always do his duty to Hilltop and to us.'

Rose nodded. She had seen that for herself. No one cared more about this place, about his duty, than Harry. 'In finding a wife?'

'Of course. Every estate needs a mistress. She would have to be the right sort, though.'

'The right sort?'

'Sensible and steady. A good, practical head on her shoulders, not like the Captain's pretty mother, rest her soul.' Mrs Perkins gave a cackling laugh. 'And rich, of course. Hilltop can't be fixed without that.'

'No,' Rose whispered. Money was the one thing she did not have to offer. 'It can't.'

Mrs Perkins peered at her closer. 'You aren't rich, are you, Miss Parker?'

'I fear not.'

'Pity.' Mrs Perkins settled back among her shawls. 'You do seem a sensible girl. Not bad looking, either.'

Rose had to laugh. 'Thank you.'

Peggy brought in the tea then, carefully balancing the heavy tray in her small hands. She was the perfect young lady as she poured out the tea and served it, and soon she and her grandmother were laughing at Rose over some of her tales of life at Aunt Sylvia's grand house.

'You all seem very merry,' Mr Perkins said as the men re-joined them. He swung his daughter up in his arms, making her giggle.

'Miss Parker was telling us such stories,' Peggy said.

'Stories?' Harry asked.

'Oh, just about my Aunt Sylvia,' Rose answered. 'No one would believe she was quite real if they had not met her!'

'Miss Parker is quite a lovely gel,' Mrs Perkins said, chuckling. 'Won't you have some tea before you go, Captain? I have a few things I'd like to ask you about the property...'

Harry had thought he knew Rose Parker well enough by then, knew her quiet thoughtfulness, her devotion to her family, all the things that made her, well, *Rose*. A lady of such subtle understanding that one was drawn to her almost without realising it, without knowing how very addictive her warmth, her smiles, could be.

But now he saw she was fun, too, as he

stood in the sitting-room doorway of that small cottage and watched her singing with little Peggy, her cheeks pink and her eyes glowing. Peggy was giggling and even her grandmother was smiling and clapping along to the song.

It was a scene of glowing, intimate happiness and Rose had created it in only a short hour. Created it because that was who she was. She could not help herself. Despite her life, her work as a companion to help her family, which could not be an easy or pleasant task for a refined lady, she still made everything about her just a bit brighter, a bit lighter.

Including himself. After the war, he had been sure he would not laugh again. But she made him want to sweep her into his arms and dance around the room with her, to protect her. And it was the hardest thing he had ever done to admit he wasn't able to.

'Now that's a fine lady,' he heard Oscar say and he turned to look at the man, somehow surprised to find he and Rose were not really the only two people in the world.

Oscar, too, watched her with a smile.

'Yes,' Harry said. 'She is.'

'I haven't seen Peggy laugh like that since we lost her mother,' Oscar said. 'The children at Barton must adore her.'

'So they do,' Harry said, thinking of Jane and Hayden's children, the way they looked at Rose as they sang, so eager for her smiling approval. The way they held her hands and laughed, as Peggy was doing now. Yes— she was a woman who brought warmth into every moment. She would surely be a fine mother.

'Captain St George!' Mrs Perkins called. 'Won't you come sit by the fire? Oscar's been keeping you out in the cold too long looking at that roof.'

Harry nodded, recalled to his duties by her words. That was what he had to do, no matter what—take care of his home, his people.

'Peggy has made the most delicious ginger cakes,' Rose said.

'And now I've learned a new song!' Peggy cried. 'Miss Parker says I'm a—a...'

'A natural singer,' Rose said.

'Cakes *and* music?' Harry said with a laugh. 'Who could say no?'

They spent a pleasant half-hour by the cottage fire, taking tea and singing, hearing a bit of the estate gossip from Mrs Perkins, who despite her age and infirmity seemed to know everything.

By the time they left, the winter-blue sky had turned quite grey and snow had started to drift down in fat, wet, white flakes. They caught on Rose's lashes and cheeks, sparkling like diamonds as she laughed.

'See? Now it really feels like Christmas,' she cried, setting her horse to galloping down the line towards Barton. 'Race you back to Barton!'

Harry laughed and spurred his horse to catch up with her. He had almost forgotten what it felt like to ride like that, set loose from anything but the speed and the lightness, the freedom. They raced through the gates of Barton, their horses neck and neck, until Harry pulled just slightly ahead of her at the front doors of the house. The snow had begun to fall in earnest, the lights of the windows like beacons of hope in a coming storm.

But Rose's smile turned even brighter. 'I vow you must be the winner, Captain St George! What is your forfeit?'

A kiss, he thought. 'I shall have to think of just the right prize, Miss Parker—Rose.'

Her smile widened, and she laughed. 'Well, I feel like the winner myself. It has been much too long since I could ride like that. The fresh air, the snow—it's all so wondrous.'

Harry dismounted and came around to help her down from the saddle. As she looked up at him, her hand on his arm, her expression turned wistful. 'Thank you for showing me your house, Harry,' she said. 'I enjoyed it so much. It made me see—well, made me see so much about you, I suppose.'

'And were you disappointed by what you saw?'

She glanced away, her cheeks turning pink until she looked like her name in truth. A pink and white, blooming Rose. 'Quite the contrary. I just…'

A groom came to take their horses, and Rose hurried up the steps into the house. Harry followed, but he found he couldn't let her go just yet, couldn't be without her until there was no choice.

'Stay with me,' he said hoarsely. 'Just for a moment?'

Rose looked startled, but she nodded and took his hand as he led her into a small, quiet, dark sitting room off the hall.

As the sitting room door clicked shut behind them, Harry took her into his arms and held her close, so close they couldn't possibly be parted. Not yet. Rose found herself wanting to seize the moment, to make it her own and never forget it. She looped her arms around his neck and closed her eyes, inhaling his scent of woodsmoke and fresh air, the faint touch of lemon, combined with the bayberry-greenness of Christmas itself. She knew those scents would always remind her of him now.

'Oh, Harry,' she whispered. She reached up and gently touched his scarred cheek, feeling its roughness under her fingers. 'I wish— I wish...'

But she couldn't say anything else. He moaned, a low, hoarse sound in the shadows, and his lips claimed hers. She went up on tiptoe to meet him, putting all she had into that kiss. It wasn't a gentle kiss, as their first had been. It was filled with desperation, passion, need, all the feelings she could not speak.

'Rose,' he whispered, his kiss trailing over her cheek, his lips warm and firm against the life-pulse beating in her temple. 'Rose, I must…'

She was suddenly frightened of what he might say, that he could take away this moment before she could grasp it. 'You don't need to talk, Harry. I know.'

'I do need to tell you,' he said. He took a step back, but still held her hands in his, the two of them tethered in the darkness. 'I've hidden from life for too long. But you, you most extraordinary, kind-hearted woman, you make me brave again.'

'You? Not brave? Never say that,' she protested. 'You fought in battle, you were horribly injured…'

'I did fight, for so many years. It was what I had to do. But when I came home to find how I had neglected Hilltop—I have hidden from life. I couldn't face that my life had changed so much.'

How life changed, so suddenly, so unexpectedly. Yes, she knew how that felt. 'Indeed it does change, I know that.'

'I know that you do. That's why I feel I can tell you, only you, about what happened to me. How I came to be here, as I am.'

He took her hand and led her to a sofa by the high, small window that gave the room its only light. Snow still drifted down outside, thicker now, enclosing them in a silent blanket of white. She went with him, as she knew she could trust him, could follow him anywhere. But she wasn't sure she could bear to hear his words, to know of the terrible pain he must have endured.

They sat down at opposite ends of the sofa, only their hands touching in the middle. 'You know I was a soldier, of course,' he said.

Rose nodded.

'I lost so many friends,' he said. 'I could not lose my home, too. Could not let people down as I did some of those friends.'

'Oh, Harry, you could never do that,' she

protested. 'I am sure you saved so many. You would never let anyone down, not at all.'

He gave her sad smile. 'Sweet Rose. You do always see the good in everyone, in everything.'

'I wish I did,' she said. 'I wish I could see—oh, Harry. We shouldn't be here like this.'

'Definitely not,' he answered roughly. But still his head bent towards hers and she instinctively leaned forward to meet him, to meet the kiss she so longed for.

The touch of his lips was soft at first, warm and gentle. When she wrapped her arms around him to draw him closer, he answered her hunger with his own and deepened the kiss. Their lips parted, tasted—and that taste sent Rose tumbling down into a new, primitive need she had never imagined before. Scandal, the past—it all meant nothing in that one perfect moment.

A moment that was all too quickly shattered when she remembered where she was, who they were. What he had tried to tell her, that his duty to his home came first, in some kind of recompense for the friends he lost in battle. In her own good honour, she could never turn him from that. She broke away from him and jumped to her feet.

'I—I should go,' she said. '*We* should go. Shouldn't we?'

'Rose…'

She shook her head. The house was still quiet as Rose stepped into the hall, Harry close behind her. She was intently aware of his nearness, the warmth of him that always seemed to hold her secure when he was close to her.

The housekeeper Hannah came out to take their cloaks and hats.

'Have Lord and Lady Ramsay returned, Hannah?' Rose asked, self-consciously smoothing her hair as she took off her hat.

'Yes, quite a time ago,' Hannah answered with a sniff. 'And the others are dressing for dinner. Shall I have water sent up for a bath, Miss Parker?'

Rose was suddenly aware of just how long she had been alone with Harry. Being with him just seemed to make her forget all else, but she knew she couldn't do that. She had to be careful. 'Yes, thank you, Hannah.'

As the housekeeper vanished and Rose turned towards the stairs, Harry reached for her hand. 'You won't forget, Rose?'

She shook her head. 'I won't forget.' She felt him watching her all the way up the stairs.

Chapter Twelve

'What is this, then?' Mrs Pemberton cried as her long-suffering maid, Miss Powell, put her breakfast tray carefully across her velvet and lace-covered knees.

'Tea, madam. And toast with marmalade. As usual.' Powell had been with Mrs Pemberton for years and knew how every morning proceeded. She calmly crossed the floor to open the window curtains and let in the pale grey winter light.

'But what is *this*?' Mrs Pemberton picked up a small pile of letters and waved them around. The lace cap perched on her white curls trembled.

'The morning post, madam.' Powell stirred at the fire the housemaid had laid in the pre-dawn gloom.

'Why does anyone persist in writing to me?' Sylvia grumbled. 'It's probably just the usual begging letters from my useless relatives. Vultures and bores, the lot of them.' She took a sip of her tea and thought of her relatives. She had married well when she was quite young and he quite old, and as they had no children and his estate was not entailed and very extensive, she had lived a most comfortable life, one she looked back on now with much satisfaction.

But now that she was old, cousins and step-cousins and grand-cousins she never even knew she possessed seemed to come out of the woodwork.

Sylvia sighed and leaned back on her piles of lace-trimmed pillows. Growing old was no game for the weak, she saw that every day now in hearing that was fading, energy flagging. She had to take her enjoyment where she could. It was amusing in its own way to dangle those relatives along a bit.

But sometimes it was merely wearying. The grand house was so quiet now, so unlike the days when she was young and the corridors were filled with parties, with friends and lovers and fun. She had seized it all with both hands and made the most of being pretty and rich. She regretted not a moment of it.

But what to do now? How to leave her mark on the world?

She took another sip of tea and frowned to find it had gone cold. Rose would never have allowed such a thing. Rose had a quick, quiet efficiency about her that made Sylvia's life so comfortable, so easy. So much less lonely.

Sylvia had to admit it, even if it was only to herself—she missed Rose. The girl rather reminded her of herself when she was very young, straightforward and practical and un-apologetic in a way young ladies did not seem to be in the modern world. Sylvia had been willing to do whatever she could to help her family, her mother and sisters, and so was Rose. Sylvia had married well; Rose looked after Sylvia. And Sylvia knew herself quite well enough to see Rose had a harder bargain to keep than she herself ever had.

Rose worked so her pretty, silly sister could marry her handsome, poor curate. If only there was a curate out there for Rose.

Or better, a rich husband like the one Sylvia herself once snagged.

Sylvia laughed. No, she couldn't quite wish that on such a sweet girl as Rose. Sylvia had known how to ruthlessly get her way with an old husband; Rose would be too kind.

'I think there is a letter from Miss Parker,' Powell said, as if she read her employer's thoughts. 'I do hope she is enjoying herself at Barton.'

Sylvia sorted through the post, trying to conceal her eagerness. There was indeed a missive at the bottom of the pile marked with Rose's neat hand.

She opened it and quickly scanned the lines. 'It sounds as if Jane is indeed making a merry holiday this year. And Rose says the children are quite talented with their music.'

'She must be glad to be there, then,' Powell said with a sigh, laying out Sylvia's morning gown. 'We do miss her here, though.'

'Yes. I suppose we do. None of you has her droll way of reading aloud.' Sylvia watched as Powell smoothed the creases from a grey-velvet gown and ruffled shawl. 'Whatever is *that*?'

'Your morning gown, madam,' Powell said. 'Unless you don't feel like going downstairs until later?'

'Of course I will go downstairs! I'm old, not ill. But no one will see or care how I'm dressed, anyway.' She thought for a moment about the Christmases she used to see in that house, the music and games. She glanced back down at Rose's letter.

Something among the descriptions of dinners and games caught her attention. Rose mentioned a certain name not once, not twice, but three times, and in a way that was clear she hadn't even realised it.

Captain Harry St George. Going for rides, showing them his house, sledding parties. Sylvia remembered the young man well, a war hero and certainly no fool as so many young people were. Now gossip said he was quite scarred, a recluse at his crumbling estate at Hilltop. But Rose did not make him sound that way at all.

Sylvia tapped the letter thoughtfully on the edge of her tray, a thought slowly taking form in her mind.

'Powell,' she said. 'Have the footmen bring

down my trunks and for heaven's sake find something I own that isn't grey or black. It is Christmas, after all.'

Powell looked up, her eyes wide. Sylvia smiled to see that she had at last truly surprised her maid. 'Madam?'

'We are going to a party,' she said, pushing the breakfast tray aside. 'We're going to Barton Park. There's something I must do.'

Chapter Thirteen

'Snapdragon! Snapdragon!'

Everyone chanted and clapped their hands as all the light except for the fireplace was extinguished in the Barton drawing room. The footmen carried in a wide, shallow bowl of brandy with raisins and other dried fruit. After it was carefully placed on the table, Hayden stepped forward to set a match to the confection.

Rose gasped as eerie blue flames flickered across the lake of brandy. She remembered watching the grown-ups play at the game when she was a child and it always seemed so daring, everyone diving through the incandescent light to snatch at the treat. She found it looked no less wondrous now, with the circle of avid, laughing faces cast in the blue glow.

The children had been sent to bed with their nurse after their pre-dinner song, led by Rose, and dinner had been an adult event with plentiful fine French wines. Even Rose, who had tried to sip very little since wine went right to her head and made her giddy, found herself giggling at the silly stories and jokes.

It had been Charles St George, in his King of the Bean guise, who declared cards and charades too dull for the after-dinner entertainment and instead sent for the brandy. He led the cheers as the flames danced higher.

Rose glimpsed Harry across the flames, his face half-hidden in the shadows. He smiled wryly as he watched his brother. She remembered all too well their kiss, the wondrous way it had made her feel, and now her cheeks grew warm at the memory. She told herself it was merely the fire, and not her old nemesis, her blush.

'Since you are the ruler of the evening, Charlie,' said Helen Fallon, the diamond stars in her hair glittering in the firelight, 'you must be the first to try.'

'And so I shall,' Charles answered. 'If the prize is a kiss from the fairest lady in the room.'

Helen and Charles exchanged a long, tense glance and Rose saw that Harry watched them with a small frown. Lady Fallon was an heiress and had once been almost engaged to Harry. Surely now...

No, Rose told herself as she made herself concentrate on the game. It was not her business. Yet she was much too aware of what Harry and his brother and Lady Fallon did.

'I doubt Jane would oblige you,' Helen said, turning away as if she cared not a jot what happened.

Jane laughed. 'It is not *that* kind of party, my darlings, whether the children are in their nursery or not. But, yes, Charlie, you must be the first. I see a lovely little apricot just there in the middle...'

Amid cries of encouragement, Charles dived forward to try and snatch the apricot. He was unsuccessful and fell back shaking his hand. Helen laughed. Hayden went next and managed to grab a raisin and pop it between his wife's lips.

Harry was next and he took the prize of the apricot with such ease it looked as if he barely moved. As he flung the fruit into his mouth, the tips of his fingers seemed to drip with the blue flame. In the strange, glowing light, he looked like something magical and fascinating.

Emma stepped forward to try it. She gave a little shriek, but managed to grab a raisin. 'It's hot, but it doesn't burn,' she declared. 'How is that possible?'

After the flames died down and the brandy cooled, the lanterns were lit again and the world shifted back to its everyday appearance. Rose laughed with the others, trying not to look at Harry.

'What shall we do now?' Jane said. 'Charles, you are the guide to our merriment and obviously a very good one. What game do you declare?'

Charles tapped his chin in thought. 'I say—hide and go seek.'

Helen clapped her hands. 'Wonderful! Who shall hide and who shall seek?'

'The ladies shall hide and the gentlemen seek, of course,' Charles said. 'Is that not the way of life? Jane, perhaps you will be time-keeper?'

Jane glanced at her husband. She looked a bit dubious about the new game, but she nodded and smiled. 'Just no hiding in the nursery wing. My children are too excited over Christmas to sleep as it is.'

'Very well, ladies,' Charles said. 'Get ready, get set—hide!'

Rose was caught in the midst of the crowd rushing out of the drawing room, carried with them into the hall as Jane counted off behind them. 'One—two—three…' she called, her voice floating above the giggles. Everyone scattered up the stairs and vanished into the shadows, leaving only the trace of that laughter and faint, flowery perfumes behind.

Rose wasn't sure where to go. She hadn't played the game since she was a child and even then she had usually just found a quiet corner to read in.

'Nineteen, twenty,' Jane called and Rose knew she didn't have much time. She ran up the stairs and turned down the first corridor she saw. It was only lit by flickering lights at each end, in between was shadows. She heard giggles nearby, the snap of closing doors. Suddenly rather nervous, she ducked behind some heavy satin curtains into a small window nook and pressed herself tight against the wall.

But she was not alone there for long. After a few breathless moments, someone slid between the curtains and joined her.

It was shadowy in her small sanctuary, but in the moonlight she could see it was Harry who stood there, his tall figure glowing in the phosphorescent light, his scars hidden. He stepped closer to her, letting the velvet curtain fall behind him, and they were alone in their own world.

Rose found she suddenly wasn't frightened at all. She was no longer all by herself. She could take a breath, a *real* breath, at last.

'Rose?' he asked, his voice quiet and deep, as rich and comforting as a velvet blanket. 'Are you unwell? You ran away so quickly...'

'I—no. Not at all,' she answered. 'It's just the game—suddenly I couldn't breathe.'

'I don't like such things myself,' he said. 'The darkness, the sudden noise.'

Rose swallowed hard, remembering the little he had told her about the horrors of battle. How dreadful that silly Christmas games could bring that back to him. She longed to touch him, to comfort him. 'Of course not.'

'It seems safe enough here.'

'Yes.' Rose swayed towards him, drawn by that warm, quiet strength she always found so wondrous, by the delicious winter fire scent of him.

His arms came out to catch her, drawing her close, and suddenly she did not feel safe at all. She felt her heart racing within her, making her feel reckless and full of something she hadn't known in so long—joy.

She rested her forehead against his chest, the soft wool of his evening coat warm on her skin. She closed her eyes and concentrated on the sound of his heartbeat, steady and strong, echoing her own.

In her life, she always seemed to be rushing ahead to the next moment, to worrying about the next day. Would her mother and Lily be well? Would she be able to live com-

fortably, safely? With Harry, in that one instant, she could just *be*, and it was a delicious
feeling indeed.

She knew she should not be there alone
with him, that it was dangerous indeed, but
she couldn't give it up just yet. She slid her
arms around his waist, feeling the strength
of him as he held her up.

She felt his kiss on the top of her head and
she tilted her face up to his. His gaze glowed
in the darkness. His lips touched her brow,
the pulse that beat at her temple, her cheek,
leaving tiny touches of warmth that made
her tingle all the way to her toes. She shivered with the force of emotion that flowed
through her, like a flame that pushed away
all the icy loneliness she had lived with for
so long.

She went up on tiptoe, holding him even
closer, and at last his lips touched hers. A
small, questing, sweet kiss, but it made that
flame burn even brighter. She moaned softly
and it seemed the small sound ignited something in him, too. He groaned and dragged
her so close there was nothing between them

at all. They seemed to fit together perfectly, as if they had always been just like that.

Her lips instinctively parted under his kiss and his tongue lightly touched the tip of hers, as if seeking, questioning, before he deepened their touch.

She wound her arms around his neck, her fingers curling into his hair, as if she could hold him to her for ever. But he wasn't leaving her. Their kiss slid deeper, into a desperate need she hadn't even known was in her. She felt so hot, as if she would catch fire from it, and all there was in the world was the touch of his kiss. She swayed, sure she would fall.

He pressed her back against the wall and his lips trailed from hers, over the arch of her throat to touch the tiny hollow where her life-pulse pounded with need.

'Rose, I...' he gasped hoarsely. She opened her eyes to find that he rested his forehead against the wall beside her. His breath was ragged in her ear, his tall body shuddering as if he struggled with the force of longing just as she did.

Suddenly, the world seemed to crash in

around their little sanctuary. She heard footsteps and muffled laughter from beyond the curtains.

She feared that if she stayed so close to him, she wouldn't be able to think at all. She slid to one side, dizzy, but his arms tightened around her.

'Not yet,' he growled. 'Please.'

Rose nodded and leaned against his shoulder, letting him hold her up. His entire body had gone rigid, perfectly still, as if he fought to regain his military control.

''Tis an enchantment,' she whispered. 'Like the spirits in the holly wreath, or *A Midsummer Night's Dream*.'

He gave a ragged laugh. 'We need Puck's remedy to set it right.'

It *did* feel like something had been set loose in Rose, something wild she had never known before. She also knew it had to be put back in the bottle before their lives were cast adrift. She could not afford gossip, not if she was to keep her position, and he needed an heiress.

'Tomorrow is Christmas Day,' she said. 'They say that is a good time for reflection and correction.'

He turned his head to look at her and she saw a small smile crook the corner of his lips. 'Oh, my sweet Rose. I think I would need more than one Christmas Day at this point.'

Rose shook her head. 'I know you. Your mistakes can surely not be many.'

He laughed roughly. 'They are many indeed. If you knew what my youth was like before the army…'

Rose heard more voices outside, laughter becoming louder, closer. She shivered with the sudden rush of cold reality and edged away from Harry, even as her whole being urged her to stay, stay, stay. She self-consciously smoothed her skirt, her hair.

It was as if mad holiday spirits had indeed taken over her world, a place she had always fought to keep so ordered and calm. She didn't *want* to go back, but she knew she had to. For both their sakes.

She slipped out of their little alcove and blinked at the sudden glow of the light. She saw that many of the hiders had been found and a crowd was drifting down the stairs. She followed them into the drawing room where

Jane played at the pianoforte while several couples danced.

'Miss Parker!' little Eleanor cried, rushing out of the crowd in her dressing gown. Rose was glad of the feeling of the girl's hand on hers, an anchor to the real world. 'There you are.'

'And there you are,' Rose answered with a shaky laugh. She saw William and the other children were gathered around their father, being swung into the air in time to the music, making them shout with laughter. 'Shouldn't you all be in bed?'

'We wanted to see what you were doing, if you would sing for us since it's so hard to sleep on Christmas Eve,' Eleanor said with a winsome smile.

Rose remembered that feeling so well, when she and Lily would stay up long into the darkness, whispering about what treats might wait for them in the morning. 'Very well. Just one song, though. Tomorrow will be a long day.'

She clasped Eleanor's hand and led her upstairs, trying to forget what had happened under the enchantment of the game. She feared it would be a sleepless night indeed.

Helen tiptoed across the upstairs landing, listening carefully to the muffled whispering and laughter of the game. She could see no one in the shadows, nor did she really want to. She tripped over one of the rugs and caught herself before she could fall, laughing at the rush of uncertainty that ran through her. She hadn't felt that way in so very long, so unsure, so filled with anticipation of the next few moments, whatever they would bring.

But she was not quite alone. Behind her, she heard the brush of a footstep, the sound of an indrawn breath, almost nothing in the silence.

'Who is there?' she called out, her heart pounding.

A tall figure stepped out of the shadows and as her eyes adjusted to the moonlight she saw it was Charles. He held a goblet of brandy loose in his hand and she remembered how he had urged them all on in their silly holiday games. He did not look so merry now. In fact, he looked quite—solemn.

'Oh, it's you,' she said and she turned to run away again. But somehow she could not leave him. She didn't want to leave him. She glanced back at him uncertainly.

A wry smile touched his lips and he raised his glass again. 'Yes, only me. Are you so very disappointed, Helen?'

'Not at all. I merely heard laughter from this direction and wondered if Jane's children had escaped their nursery.'

'Or maybe it's the ghosts of Barton, come to haunt our feast?'

'Are there ghosts here? It seems too new a house to be haunted.' But then again, her fine London house was quite new and she felt as if ghosts followed her around there all the time. The ghost of her husband, the ghost of the wild girl she had once been.

'There are ghosts everywhere, as I'm sure you know. Especially at Christmas. That's when we remember those lost ones the most.'

Helen sat down on the nearest chair, suddenly weary. 'I thought the men were meant to be seeking, not hiding in here.'

'I prefer the quiet for the moment, don't you? You don't seem to be hiding very effectively.'

'Maybe I don't want to be found.'

'Not by anyone?'

Helen thought about that, about the gentlemen guests, some of whom she knew would welcome an invitation from her. About the hopes she had dared have for Harry before she arrived at Barton, how she wanted to bring the past to life, even when it was obviously cold and distant. 'Tell me about the Christmas ghosts.'

Charles sat down next to her and politely offered her the brandy. She had always liked that about Charles. He was so much fun at a party, but he knew how to be quiet, too, how not to press a person to talk about confusing or hurtful things. He could just—be. She had almost forgotten what that was like. With her husband, and now in her widowhood, it was always play-acting. The tales Charlie told her now, though—they felt different. She could listen to him all evening, but his words ended far too soon.

Helen took a sip of the brandy as his words

faded around them, leaving only the chilly silence of the night outside the windows of their sanctuary.

'I like that,' she said. 'Ghosts of Christmas.'

'It's not the usual sort of Christmas tale,' he answered.

'That's why I like it. Sometimes it's much too easy to feel sad at this time of year, isn't it? And all the tinsel and bows make it worse, somehow.'

Charles looked at her sharply and she could tell she had surprised him. 'The lovely Lady Fallon, sad?' he said softly. 'What is it that makes you so?'

She shrugged. 'I don't even know. What *could* make me sad? I'm a rich widow now and still young. Yet I feel so alone sometimes. That's why I like the thought of your ghosts, I suppose. If they are watching—well, they're company.'

He reached up to toy with the lace trim on her sleeve. Usually when a man did that, she would laugh and turn away flirtatiously. It would mean nothing, less than nothing. But this was Charles, Charles who had known her for so long, who felt as if she herself was seeing for the first time. She could see her own feelings, her loneliness and uncertainty, in his eyes.

His touch on her arm was so light, but to Helen it burned with the glow of life itself. She found herself craving that touch so much.

'Tell me no, Helen,' he said in a low, taut voice. 'Send me away, for both of us.'

'I...' she whispered. 'I can't do that, Charlie.'

'Heaven help me, but neither can I.' His hand trailed over her arm to her waist, his touch warm and gentle through the velvet of her gown. It made her want so much more, to feel bare skin against hers again, to have that connection, to know she was not alone.

Her throat felt so tight she couldn't answer him in words. She just covered his hand with hers and pressed him closer. His other hand reached up to caress her cheek and she kissed his palm. He smelled of smoke and brandy, and it was enough to make her head whirl. There was only her and Charlie, in their own world now.

'Helen,' he said roughly. 'Every time I think I know you, you change. You're so merry, then so sad. How you baffle me.'

'But surely you know me better than anyone else ever has. I think—I think you see me.' She leaned closer to him and felt the heat of their lips hovering mere inches apart. 'And I see you.'

'I do hope not.'

She nodded and, before she could let her thoughts overwhelm her again, she closed the space between them and touched his lips with hers. The merest brush, but she felt the heat of their breath meeting and mingling, binding them closer than those ghosts could ever do.

Charles groaned and deepened their kiss, giving her what she craved. His arms came around her, pulling her close. His tongue touched the curve of her lower lip, light and almost teasing, until she parted her lips in eager welcome. And then, like the ghosts, she flew free.

'Helen,' he growled. Through the blurry heat of her desire, she felt his touch tighten, until there was nothing between them at all.

Their kiss slid over a precipice into something wild and frantic with need that had been bottled up inside of her for too long. It was something she so longed for—and something she was afraid to have. Feeling like the veriest coward, she broke away from him and ran as fast as she could. She didn't even know where she was going, only that she had to escape herself.

Chapter Fourteen

"'I saw three ships come sailing in, come sailing in, come sailing in! I saw three ships come sailing in on Christmas Day in the morning!'"

Rose followed behind the children as they walked to church for Christmas morning services, processing behind their parents with the rest of the guests and the household around them. She tried to pay attention, to make quite sure they sang in the way they had practised so carefully, but she found her attention was always wandering.

She had barely slept a wink after that kiss with Harry, a kiss that felt like a dream now, something that surely couldn't have happened to her in real life. Not quiet, sensible Rose. And yet it *had* happened and she knew she could never forget how it made her feel. She peeked over her shoulder to where Harry walked with his brother, the two of them talking together quietly. His wide-brimmed hat shielded his expression from her view, but she couldn't help but wonder if he also remembered.

How could she leave this magical Barton Christmas world and go back to Aunt Sylvia? She knew she had to, and soon, but not quite yet.

'You children do sing so beautifully,' Emma said. 'I'm sure the congregation will love it, too. Just remember—it's Christmas, so best behaviour. We don't want a repeat of last Easter, do we?'

Rose's full attention was finally captured, wondering what on earth had happened last Easter! The Barton Park brood seemed such an angelic one, in the grand scheme of children's behaviour, anyway.

'You were the one who told us to try it, Aunt Emma,' William said. 'You said they used a special lemon polish at the holidays.'

'You said that you and Mama used to lick the pews to test it, too,' Eleanor said.

'Well, do as I say and not as I do,' Emma said airily with a wave of her gloved hand. 'No more licking of pews this year, or there shall be no plum pudding at dinner for you.'

'I would never do such a thing,' Beatrice said. 'Yuck!'

'Of course you would not, Bea,' said Emma. 'You are quite an angel.'

'Not entirely an angel!' William protested. 'Was she not the one who got lost looking for the treasure?'

'Arabella's treasure?' Rose asked. 'When were you lost, Miss Marton?'

Beatrice's delicate cheeks turned bright pink. 'A long time ago. I was just a silly child. And I never found it, anyway. I am sure it doesn't exist.'

'It does!' William declared. 'We just have to narrow its location more carefully. It's somewhere over there, near the old ruins on Uncle David's estate.' He waved towards the shadow of a crumbling old chimney in the distance.

'If it *did* exist, it could certainly be helpful,' Emma said. She gestured with her fur-trimmed muff towards the semi-rusted gates of Hilltop, barely glimpsed in the distance, opposite the old ruins. 'You visited Hilltop, did you not, Rose? What did you think?'

'It was a fine old house,' Rose said carefully. 'Very medieval, like something in a story.'

'Yes. It just needs a bit of care, as Barton once did.' Emma glanced back, and Rose followed her stare to see that Harry walked with Lady Fallon now, that lady's hand on his arm as she whispered something to him. Their faces looked most solemn. 'There are tidier ways to see to necessities than digging in the dirt for lost treasure. A fine marriage, maybe? Harry certainly deserves it.'

Rose resolutely faced forward, willing herself not blush. 'He is a good gentleman indeed.'

Their little procession turned down the lane leading towards the village and the church. The solid, square stone Norman tower stretched up towards the grey sky as the bells tolled to summon everyone to Christmas. A large crowd had gathered in the churchyard amid the tilting old headstones, waiting to make their way into the warmth of the sanctuary.

To Rose's delighted surprise, she glimpsed a familiar face standing in the doorway. Her sister, Lily, clad in a pale green pelisse, bouncing up on her toes to study the new-comers. She held her husband's arm, as he stood beside her in his clerical robes, greet-ing the parishioners.

'Lily!' Rose cried. 'And Mr Hewlitt. How wonderful to see you! Whatever are you doing here?'

She rushed forward and Lily threw her-self into her arms. Her sister was as she al-ways had been, as delicate and sweet as a bird, smelling of lilacs. It made Rose think of home and family, and that bittersweet miss-ing of it all again.

'He's been invited to say the Christmas service here, by the bishop himself,' Lily said proudly, standing back to take her shyly smil-ing husband's arm. 'We must go home very soon, as Mama is taking care of the chil-dren for us and I fear they will run her quite ragged. But Jane has insisted we stay at Bar-ton for a few nights, as a grand treat.'

'I thought it would be a delightful holiday surprise for you, Rose,' Jane said with a laugh.

'And so it is,' Rose answered happily, drinking in the sweet sight of her sister. 'How fares Mama and the children, then?'

'They are all quite well and miss you very much. I fear I am not such a good help to them as you are and cannot take your place,' Lily said. She leaned closer and whispered, 'Hewlitt has been shown such favour of late by the bishop, I am sure he will be given a fine parish of his own soon, with a substantial vicarage and larger income. Then we can all live together again!'

Live with her family again and not worry about their safety at every moment? It sounded like an impossibly beautiful dream. 'Oh, Lily, I do hope so.'

More parishioners came along the path, claiming Mr Hewlitt's and Lily's attentions, and Rose led her charges to their place in the front pews, making sure no one licked the carved, lemon-polished wood. As they filed into their seats, she glimpsed the Perkins family, Harry's kind tenants, and waved at them. They waved back, smiling, and for a moment Rose let herself feel like she belonged there, among their community. It was quite a lovely feeling.

She sat down between Eleanor and William, helping them find their place in the hymnal as the Christmas service music soared into the old church rafters and the light shone from the ancient windows on to them in a sort of blessing. She would enjoy the day while she could and always remember it.

As the congregation sang the first song and Mr Hewlitt took his place in the pulpit, the church doors opened and a blast of cold wind swept down the aisle. Rose turned with everyone else, surprised anyone would arrive so late, and gasped at the figure who stood there, swathed in a dark fur cloak and brandishing a walking stick.

'Is it a witch, Miss Parker?' Eleanor whispered, wide-eyed.

'No,' Rose whispered back. 'It is my Aunt Sylvia!'

'So lovely!' Lily said, peering into Rose's looking glass as they got ready for the Barton Christmas ball. 'I can't remember a luncheon like that in ages. All those wonderful puddings! The children will never believe me when I tell them! I shall be twenty pounds fatter when we go home.'

Rose had to laugh, for her sister, now mother of two lovely plump cherubs, was still as tiny as she had been when they last came to Barton together. Lily was a little, golden fairy in her white muslin dress trimmed with crimson and gold ribbons. 'I'm sure Jane will send them even more puddings when you leave. Her cook is wondrous at coming up with picnic hampers.'

'I'm sure she will. And hopefully next year we shall all be together to sing your music and eat our own puddings!'

Rose smiled wistfully. 'That would be wonderful.'

Lily turned to look at her, her elfin face suddenly puckered in a frown. 'Rose, dearest, you are still in your petticoat. And you look rather tired. Was it Aunt Sylvia's unexpected appearance?'

'No, not at all.' In fact, Aunt Sylvia had been rather quiet herself after church, claiming she only needed a nap and Powell would attend to her. The reason Rose was still in her petticoat was so shallow she didn't even want to tell her sister.

Rose glanced down at the gown laid out on her bed. It was her best, a forest-green satin that had been remade from an old costume of her mother's, yet she couldn't help but wish she had something a bit—prettier. Something like the lace-trimmed confections Lady Fallon wore, stylish and elegant.

'Of course,' she said, stepping into her black evening slippers. 'We mustn't be late.'

'Rose, whatever is amiss?'

Rose tried to smile, but it felt so artificial she knew Lily would know it in a moment. 'How could anything be amiss? It is Christmas!'

'I'm your sister, Rose. I can tell something is bothering you.' Lily came to her side, taking her hand as they sat together on the bed. 'Is it Aunt Sylvia showing up like that, ruining your lovely holiday away from her? That was so silly of her.'

'No, of course not. I mean—yes, Aunt Sylvia *is* a bit silly, rushing off from her warm house like that in the middle of Christmas, but she does so often make me laugh.' Rose bit her lip. 'Lily—what is it really like to be married?'

Lily's smile turned secret and satisfied, like a cat with purloined cream. 'I can't speak for any married people but myself, of course. Sometimes it is wonderful beyond belief and sometimes I just want to hit Hewlitt over the head with an inkwell. But mostly it is just—nice.' She clutched Rose's hand in hers. 'Why? Have you met someone Mama and I should know about? If so, you *must* tell me, so I can discover if he is worthy of you.'

Lily looked so fierce that Rose had to laugh. 'No, not really. Not yet.' She thought of Harry and their kiss in the shadowed alcove. She turned away so Lily couldn't see her expression. 'I just wondered.'

'If you really want to be married, Rose dearest, I am sure Hewlitt could find someone. He knows so very many churchmen from school, you know, and some of them have their own parishes now.'

Rose remembered her brother-in-law's friends from Lily's wedding, an earnest, well-scrubbed group, scrupulously polite. Nothing like Harry, who had seen so many terrible things and been so scarred by them, yet had emerged even stronger for it. 'I am quite all right, Lily, really. I could never be the perfect vicarage hostess, as you are.'

Before Lily could answer, there was a knock at the door and it opened to reveal Aunt Sylvia's maid, Powell, with a white box in her arms.

Powell always looked rather dour, as anyone who had worked for Aunt Sylvia for so long would, but she seemed to smile just a bit as she handed the box to Rose. 'A present, from Mrs Pemberton.'

Rose was shocked. 'A—a present? From my aunt? Are you quite sure?'

Powell nodded. 'She said she didn't want anyone to think she did not pay your wages on time.'

As the maid left, Lily bounced up and down on her toes. 'Oh, do open it, Rose! I am quite aching to see what it is.'

'I am, too,' Rose said, still bemused. Aunt Sylvia was not miserly in her wages, but she never gave gifts, either. Rose lifted the lid to find just what she had been wishing for—a new gown. It frothed with rose-coloured silk and creamy lace, quite the prettiest dress she had ever seen.

'Oh…' Lily sighed, gently touching the soft sleeve. 'You will surely be the most beautiful lady at the ball, Rose.'

'I doubt it,' Rose whispered. But secretly, deep in her heart, she hoped that just one person in particular might think just that.

'I suppose Aunt Sylvia isn't one hundred per cent an ogre after all,' Lily marvelled.

'Come along, Harry, won't you dance with me?' he heard Helen say, her voice sweet and fluting over the sound of the orchestra and the dancing feet. 'You've been standing here alone in the corner too long.'

Harry laughed as he turned to her, though he felt rather abashed. He thought he was well hidden there in the corner, behind a bank of Jane's potted palms and hothouse roses, but it seemed he was not so invisible after all.

In truth, he was waiting for Rose. She hadn't appeared at the party yet and in her absence the glow of the candles seemed dimmer, the music fainter. He was more eager than he cared to admit, keeping watch on the stairs for her.

'You know I'm not much of a dancer, Helen,' he said. 'Did you not have an example of that at the assembly?'

She laughed and offered him a glass of punch. The pearls in her hair and at her wrists gleamed, along with her cream and gold gown, but even she seemed muted there in the ballroom. He feared he was besotted indeed, and a fool for a lady who seemed to like him—but could not be his.

'I know no such thing, Harry,' Helen said. 'You were quite the gentlemanly partner at the assembly. And I do remember when we were children and took dance lessons together in my mother's drawing room. Charles was more adept, of course, but you never trod on my toes.'

'Such a compliment indeed!'

She gave an exaggerated pout. 'Oh, come now, Harry, it's Christmas, and I haven't had a dance at all tonight. You could do such a favour for an old friend.'

He glanced again at the stairs. There were

more arrivals crowded in the hall, but no Rose yet. And it was clear he could no longer hide there. 'Of course. Only because I know you will always forgive my clumsiness.'

They gave their empty glasses to a footman and Harry took her hand to step into the dance. Helen was as graceful and lively as she had once been at their long-ago lessons, laughing and twirling among the other guests. But every time they turned, he still couldn't help glancing at the door, waiting for a glimpse of Rose.

Helen suddenly tugged him under a bough of mistletoe hung in a doorway, its creamy berries set off by looping red ribbons. She stared up at him, her eyes wide and beautiful. Yet he felt—only a faint regret, a sadness at remembering the past. A longing to see a different, hazel pair of eyes before him, a different pair of lips parting.

'Oh, Harry,' she said, her own voice suddenly tinged with that nostalgic sadness. 'There is nothing left for us, is there?'

He shook his head. 'Helen—you know how fond I am of you…'

'Like a sister?'

'Yes,' he said gently. 'You are indeed like a sister to me, a very dear one.'

'But there is someone for whom you feel—more,' she said. 'I can tell. I am a lady of the world now, you know! Yet—I will never forget you, Harry, ever.'

She went up on tiptoe to softly press her lips to his cheek, the unscarred side which was smooth under her sudden kiss. He glanced over her head, to see that Rose had at last appeared on the stairs into the ballroom. She glowed like an angel with the soft candlelight behind her, a rose-pink gown floating softly around her, her light brown hair gathered up in loose curls with an ivory comb.

Her gaze turned to him and he smiled in a rush of joy at the sight. He instinctively took a step towards her, only to notice that her face bore no answering smile. She looked at Helen with wide eyes and he suddenly realised that he still held Helen in his arms. That she had just kissed him.

'Rose,' he called, but she had turned and fled back up the stairs, wiping away a tear with her gloved hand. A sharp pang pierced his heart. He struggled to catch up with her, but the crowd kept shifting before him, moving in a constant stream that made the stairs come in and out of sight. He saw her sister and brother-in-law, arm in arm on the lower step, but no Rose.

By the time he broke free of the crowd, she had quite vanished.

Chapter Fifteen

'Ouch!' Rose gasped as her elbow connected with the wall, shooting a sharp pain up her arm. She kept running down the narrow back stairs, though, praying no one had heard her. She desperately needed a breath of fresh air after the crowded ballroom. After seeing Harry with Lady Fallon.

At last she tumbled out into the cold night air and its crispness cleared some of the clouds from her head. The garden was quiet, though still lit by the rows of Chinese lanterns that had led guests up the drive. The house itself was golden with light, the merry music echoing around her.

'What am I doing?' Rose murmured. It wasn't like her, sensible Rose, to run out of a party into the cold night, feeling so dizzy and strange.

She shouldn't even be thinking about Harry St George at all, not romantically. She had nothing to offer him and he had to do his duty to his home. Yet she couldn't seem to help herself. Every time she was quiet for even a moment, he was there in her mind, her memories, and she feared he would be for a long time to come, even after she returned to her real life at Aunt Sylvia's.

She drifted towards a small summerhouse set in the garden, away from the main house, but still with lanterns outlining its steps. The rest of the winter garden was in darkness, and Rose thought of the children's tales of lost royal treasure. Could it really be out there somewhere, hidden, like fairy gold in a story? If so, how lovely it would be to find it, to help Harry solve all of Hilltop's troubles.

Still thinking of the treasure, Rose glimpsed a strange pile of stones near the far side of the summerhouse. They seemed out of place in the manicured garden.

She crept closer to examine them. They

seemed to fall in a tumble, as if collapsed to hide something, like the entrance to a cellar of some sort. She nudged one with the toe of her slipper, but it didn't move. She kicked it harder and tripped, falling towards the sharp stones before she could catch her balance.

She cried out and felt someone grab her arm, like a ghost coming out of the night. She shrieked, her heart seeming to fly into her throat. She whirled around—and found it was no ghost that had caught her, but Harry. He was shadowed by the luminous lamplight behind him, but she knew it was him. Her heart beat even faster, but not from fright this time.

'Blast it, Harry, you frightened me' was all she could gasp.

He gave her a rueful smile. 'I'm sorry, Rose. I thought you heard me calling you. You shouldn't be out here by yourself in the dark.'

Rose laughed. 'I—I know. I just needed a breath of fresh air.'

'I agree. It is much too crowded in there, too much noise.'

She remembered what he had told her of

his time in battle, the loud noises, the chaos, the feeling of being trapped. She reached out and gently touched his arm, hoping he knew those nightmares were no longer real, that he was not alone in a cruel, cold world. 'And I think Charles must have put something in the claret cup. I feel rather dizzy.'

Harry laughed and she was glad to see it seemed to banish some of the darkness from his eyes. 'You are right. It's just like Charles to do such a mischief. I plan to blame him entirely.' He took Rose's hand in his and she felt the warm steadiness of him envelop her until the night held no more fears. He was honourable, she knew that very well after seeing him with his tenants, hearing of his time in battle. He was a man who could be trusted, always, and she knew how rare that was.

His laughter faded and as he watched her his expression was most serious, intent. He drew her closer to him, his hands tight on her waist, and that feeling of warm safety sparked into something more. Something as shimmering and irresistible as those flickering lantern flames. It was as bright and wondrous as life itself. Not like her everyday life, grey and practical, but like a daydream come to vivid life.

She didn't want to let it go. She didn't want to lose this beauty now that she had found it.

She swayed closer to him, and wound her arms tightly around his neck so he couldn't fly away and leave her alone in this dream. She only wanted to stay here in his embrace all night—for every night, really. To forget about duty and families and treasure, and everything but him.

She gazed up at him in the moonlight, thinking how handsome he was, made even more so by his honourable scars. She had never known anyone like him at all. 'How beautiful you are, Harry,' she whispered.

He laughed in surprise. 'Of course I'm not. I was never handsome and now I'm quite a wreck.'

Rose shook her head. How could she ever convince him of what she saw, of what was true? She seemed to have no words left, her head fuzzy with the drink, the moonlight and the magic. Instead of talking, she went up on tiptoe and pressed her lips to his in a swift, sweet kiss, then another and another, as if she could never have her fill.

He groaned and pulled her closer, so close there was not even a breath of the cold night between them. He deepened the kiss, his tongue seeking the taste of hers, and she was lost completely in him. Lost in that wild need to be just that close to him, always. To draw all he was into her until they were inseparable.

For once in her life, Rose didn't question herself, didn't draw back. She trusted Harry. She knew in that one moment he would always do right by her.

He pressed tiny, fleeting kisses to her cheek, her temple, the tiny, sensitive spot behind her ear. She shivered to feel the warm rush of his breath on her skin.

'Oh, Rose,' he whispered hoarsely. 'You know we can't go on like this.'

She nodded, pressing her face into his shoulder. She tried to breathe, but that only seemed to bring the essence of him even closer, all around her. She saw now that he was the one true thing she had always hoped for, so kind and strong.

'I know we can't,' she answered. 'But I can't—I can't go back to what was before. I can't…'

She shivered and he stood back to take her hand. 'At the very least, we can't stay out here in the cold,' he said.

Rose nodded and let him lead her across the darkened garden and up the steps of the summerhouse. It was all marble, still chilly without the summer sun its stone walls usually saw, but it was out of the wind, away from anyone who might stumble out of the dance. She could see the shadow of pillars from the flickering lights outside, the outline of some wrought-iron garden furniture. It was so quiet there that she could hear her heart pounding in her ears.

She swallowed hard past her fear, past doubts. Never before had she been given the chance for a moment of such perfect happiness. She feared it would never come again. She intended to grab it now, to give herself something beautiful to remember. To be free.

Still shaking, she reached up and pulled the pins from her hair, shaking the heavy mass free over her shoulders.

As he watched her, his gaze narrowed, and she saw the quick beat of his pulse in his temple, the way his jaw tensed. 'Rose...'

'No, Harry, please.' She pressed her finger to his lips before he could say anything else. She wanted no words to shatter this spell. She was done with words, with worry and thought and being practical, even if it was only for that moment.

She sat down on the nearby iron *chaise*, drawing him with her. He wrapped his arms around her, holding her close, and she felt a burst of hope. Perhaps she was not alone. Perhaps, even though duty said they could not always be together, they *could* truly be together, just the two of them.

'I—I want you, Harry,' she managed to whisper. 'Do you want me, too?'

'Beautiful Rose. How could you ever doubt it? My feelings for you are—well, they are beyond an old soldier's words. I'm no poet. But you are the loveliest woman I have ever met.' He kissed her again, their lips meeting in a hot blur of need, and she let herself tumble into him and be lost.

She clumsily, eagerly, untied his cravat

and let it fall to the floor at their feet. Something hidden deep inside of her, something urgent and instinctive, guided her as she pushed back his coat and the soft muslin of his shirt, as she eagerly touched his bare, warm skin and marvelled at the sheer life of him.

Clinging to each other, they fell back on the *chaise*, the domed marble of the ceiling whirling over her head. She rolled on top of him, not able to breathe as she studied him in the moonlight. His bare skin seemed gilded. How glorious he was, vibrant with desire and strength. It was beyond her dreams.

Her trembling fingertips traced the light, coarse sprinkling of dark hair on his chest, the thin line that led tantalisingly to the band of his velvet evening breeches. His stomach muscles tightened, his breath turning ragged as her touch brushed against it.

'Rose, my darling,' he gasped. 'Be careful. If you're not sure about me…'

'I would not be here if I wasn't sure,' she answered and she suddenly realised how very sure she was. This, him—it was the most right thing she had ever done.

She fell back into his arms, their lips meeting, heartbeats melding. There was nothing careful about that kiss, it was as hot as the sun and full of urgent, desperate need, like fireworks bursting into the night sky. She felt the slide of his hands on her back as he unlaced her gown. The winter air was cold on her skin, but she barely noticed it. Clothes were only a barrier now between her and the touch of his bare hand on her skin. She shrugged her gown away, pushing with it any last remnants of shyness.

'Rose,' he groaned, his hands tightening on her hips, warm through the thin muslin of her petticoat. 'You are so beautiful.'

How she hoped she was, for him. She kissed him again and he rolled her body beneath his, on to his discarded evening coat. She laughed as her hair spilled all around them. She *did* feel beautiful as he looked at her, felt free at last, as she knew she would when with him! There was only now, this one moment, where she was with the man she loved. Yes, *loved*, for she knew her heart was Harry's and no one else's. He kissed her and all other thoughts vanished.

She closed her eyes, and let herself revel in the feelings his touch created, the press of his kiss on her bare skin. Her palms slid over his back, so strong and warm, sheltering her under his strength. Her legs parted as she felt his weight lower between them and a new sensation she had never even imagined.

She knew what happened; she had been out in the world too long to be an ignorant miss. But the knowledge of *how* had never told her how it would *feel*, the heady, dizzy sensation of falling, falling, caught by another person and held above the world.

'I don't—don't want to hurt you,' he gasped. 'But I can't wait any longer.'

Rose smiled as she felt the press of him against her, the way her whole body ached and tingled for that final union that meant she was his, even if he could never truly be hers. 'You never could.'

She spread her legs a bit wider and he slid into her, making them as one. It did hurt a bit, a quick, burning pain, but it was nothing to the way it felt when he was joined with her. She arched her back, wrapping her arms and legs around him so tightly he could never escape her.

'You see?' she whispered against his hair as he leaned into her shoulder. 'I am completely perfect.'

'My beautiful Rose,' he gasped. Slowly, so slowly, he moved again within her, drawing back, edging forward, a little more intimate each time. Rose closed her eyes tightly, feeling all the ache ebb away until there was only pleasure. A tingling delight grew and expanded inside of her heart, warming like the sun. She had never known or even imagined anything like it.

She cried out at the wonder of it all, at the bursts of light she saw behind her closed eyes, all blue and white and gold. The heat of it was too much. How could she survive without being consumed completely?

Above her, all around her, she felt his body grow tense, his back arch. 'Rose!' he shouted out.

She flew apart, she clung to him and let herself fall down into the fire and be consumed.

After long moments, she slowly opened her eyes, wondering if she really had fallen deep into some volcano. But it was only the summerhouse, still that pale marble in the winter moonlight.

But she was not the same. That wondrous sparkle still followed her and she held on to it with all her strength.

Beside her, collapsed on to the *chaise* with his arms tight around her, was Harry. He seemed to be asleep, his breath harsh, his limbs sprawled out in exhaustion.

Rose smiled at the sight and felt herself slowly, so slowly, floating back down to earth. She felt the iron of the *chaise* beneath his coat, the soreness of her body. But none of that mattered. Nothing mattered but this moment out of time. She had become someone different in his arms, someone beautiful and bold. Or maybe, just maybe—she had become her truest self.

Rose hardly dared to breathe as she watched Harry in the moonlight. Asleep, he looked so very young, so free of any bad memories or worries. He had a faint smile on his lips, as if his dreams were good ones. A lock of his dark hair curled on his brow.

She gently smoothed it back, marvelling at his beauty, like a warrior king in slumber. She couldn't believe what they had just done together, been to each other. It already seemed like a beautiful dream, lost in the mists, beyond her grasp. She lightly traced her fingertip across his cheek, feeling the warmth of his skin under her touch.

She didn't want to leave him. There was a physical ache inside of her, as if snapping that new, tender bond was a wound. But she knew she had to do it. She would be missed at the party if she was gone much longer, and the longer she stayed with him the harder it would be to leave.

She leaned over and pressed a soft kiss to his lips. He sighed and rolled over, but did not awaken.

'Sleep now, my love,' she whispered. Hopefully when he woke again, he would also remember their time together as a sweet dream. She tucked his coat closer around him and stood to straighten her gown and make sure her hair was once more pinned into place. She did not feel like the old Rose at all, but she had to look like her once more. She had to hide that new glow deep in her heart, keep it only her own secret.

She tiptoed to the door and could not resist a look back over once more. He still slept there, so peacefully, his face so beautifully sculpted in the shadows. She blew him a kiss and slipped out into the night.

The cold wind swept around her, as if it tried to extinguish that summer-warm glow once and for all, but Rose was determined not to let it. She hurried across the garden and up the shallow steps to the terrace of the Barton drawing room. Through the tall glass windows she glimpsed the dancers, a jewel-like mosaic of bright satins and velvets under the golden light of hundreds of candles. She could hear the faint strains of music and the patter of dancing feet, and now *they* seemed like the dream. The noise and light seemed unreal, harsh.

Rose hesitated for a moment outside, watching the crowd sweep by. Aunt Sylvia sat near the fireplace, where Lily and her husband chattered with her. Aunt Sylvia frowned as she, too, studied the crowd, tapping her walking stick impatiently, but she didn't seem to need Rose yet. Rose glanced back over her shoulder, hoping to glimpse the summerhouse, but it was hidden among the trees. She only had one way to go—forward, alone.

One of the glass doors opened and Lady Fallon slipped outside, all golden and crimson, glowing with rubies. She didn't seem to see Rose at first at first and as Rose watched her bright smile fade away she looked so much older, harder, than the usual stylish lady of society she usually appeared. She glided over to the marble balustrade and opened her beaded reticule.

To Rose's shock, Lady Fallon brought out a thin, dark cheroot and lit it, a tiny beacon of light in the night. Rose had never seen a lady do such a thing. But her shock faded quickly. Of course Lady Fallon went her own way. She had the beauty and the money to be independent, to make many of her own choices. Rose quite envied her for that.

Yet she didn't envy the sad look that shadowed Lady Fallon's eyes as she studied the garden. Or the fact that, with all that money and independence, she could so easily give

Harry what he needed, what Rose herself could not.

Rose tried to slip behind her and unobtrusively go back into the ballroom, but Lady Fallon noticed her. Her eyes widened for an instant, as if in surprise, then went back into her brilliant, blinding social smile.

'Miss Parker,' she said. 'I thought I was alone out here.'

'I just needed a breath of fresh air,' Rose answered, hoping she did not sound too breathless, did not look dishevelled.

'Indeed. Jane holds such lovely parties, but sometimes they do get so—noisy.' Lady Fallon offered her the silver case.

Rose shook her head, though she was quite tempted to give it a try. 'This all must seem quite small next to grand London balls.'

'Not at all. I think Jane knows everyone within a hundred miles, and they all want to be at her soirées. Sometimes I do think—' She broke off.

'Think what, Lady Fallon?' Rose asked, curious.

'That I would like to know what a small,

cosy family Christmas would be like. I don't think I've ever known such a thing.'

Rose was surprised. Lady Fallon did not seem like the 'small, cosy family' sort of anything. 'I did always love Christmas when my sister and I were small.'

'Did you?' Lady Fallon gave her a curious glance. 'What did you and your family do?'

'Oh, nothing too exciting. Games, walks to church, gifts like dolls and sweets. My father would give us piggyback rides and sometimes Lily and I would see our parents try to sneak a kiss under the mistletoe,' Rose said wistfully, remembering those long-ago days when all seemed so safe and sweet.

Lady Fallon sighed. 'Lovely.'

Rose nodded. Maybe Lady Fallon would be good for Harry after all and not just her money. Maybe she could help him build a family for Hilltop. 'I should go find my aunt before she misses me.'

'Of course.' Lady Fallon studied the dark garden again and Rose slipped back into the drawing room. She made her way through the crowd, which was growing ever more lively as the claret cup punch flowed and the music wound louder.

She found her way to Aunt Sylvia and Lily gave her a relieved smile. 'There you are at last, Rose,' Sylvia grumbled. 'You have quite been neglecting me. I am in need of a glass of wine.'

'Of course, Aunt,' Rose said with a rueful laugh. Her dream was quite over. 'I shall not be so neglectful again.'

Chapter Sixteen

'You are looking disgustingly cheerful this morning,' Charles grumbled as Harry joined him at the Barton breakfast table.

'Do I?' Harry said with a laugh. He *did* feel rather good-humoured, better than he had in a very long time. Perhaps better than ever before. And it was all thanks to Rose. Sweet, wondrous Rose.

When he had awakened in the chilly night to find her gone, he had felt most bereft. He wanted to tear out of the summerhouse and find her, to take her in his arms and declare that he would never let her leave his side again. That he could not be without her, now that he had finally found her, and the world shone brighter than he ever knew it could.

War, the past—it was gone, melted away in the warmth of her kiss.

But he still knew she was right to go, so as not to cause a scandal. He never wanted her to think he had been forced to propose to her when he desperately wanted her by his side for all the years to come. Not because of what had happened between them in the summerhouse, but only for herself. He could no longer envision a life without her.

So he had dressed and made his way back out into the night, but he didn't return to the party. He couldn't face the crowd and the noise, and he was sure he wouldn't be able to see Rose there and *not* kiss her, not reveal to everyone there that she was his. Instead he took a long walk in the cold, deserted gardens, trying to make a plan to move forward in his life. To fulfil his duty with Rose beside him.

He hadn't slept at all, yet he felt bursting with energy. He felt—was it? Could it be happiness? It was a strange sensation and a very pleasant one.

As he ate his breakfast eggs, he studied his brother across the table. Everyone else was still in bed or enjoying the clear, sunny morning with the last of the snow, and they were alone, as they had so often been as children. Unlike himself, his brother did *not* look as if he was filled with lightness and hope. Charles's face was pale, his hair rumpled and he nursed a strong cup of tea with only uneaten toast on his plate. Harry frowned with a new worry. He needed Charles's help if the future was to work as he hoped. He wanted his brother to find such happiness, too.

'I suppose I do feel in fine fettle this morning,' Harry said. 'But you look exhausted.'

Charles shrugged. 'It's nothing at all. Just a surfeit of Christmas.'

Harry nodded. It *had* been a delightful holiday at Barton, filled with music and laughter and games, with friends all around. Surely it was the perfect setting to find unexpected love. But also to indulge in too much wine. He hoped that was all it was for Charles.

'What would you think if I went into the army again this year?' he asked as he buttered his toast.

Charles's eyes widened and he sat up

straight in surprise. 'The army, Harry? Whatever for?'

'It is only an idea,' Harry said. And perhaps the only idea that would work for now. He could make some money in the army, to send home, and Charles could look after Hilltop. With Rose as Harry's wife, she would also have a home there, a place as its mistress. Harry had seen how kind she was with his tenants, how she shared his vision of a prosperous estate for them all. It would not be as quick a solution as Charles's idea of marrying an heiress, but it was something of a plan. A beginning for them all.

He wondered what Rose would think of it and could only hope she would agree. That she would take him despite everything.

'I know I can't fight any longer,' he said. 'A one-eyed, scarred officer is no good on a battlefield. But I have much experience with strategy, too, and with the logistics of moving armies. I am sure such experience could be valuable.'

'But why would you want to do that?'

'To earn an income, of course.'

Charles shook his head, as if he could not

believe what he was hearing. 'What of marrying well?'

'I do plan to marry well,' he answered
carefully. 'But she has no great fortune.'

'You mean—you are betrothed? But to
whom?' Charles asked. 'To Miss Parker?'

Harry glanced at the door to make sure
they were still alone. 'Yes, though I have not
formally asked her yet. You must keep it to
yourself for the moment.'

'Of course. I do like Miss Parker and she
would suit you very well. Yet—' He broke
off and shook his head.

'Yet what, Charlie?'

'What about Helen?'

'Oh, Charlie. Any chance Helen and I
might have had was gone long ago and that
is for the best. We would never have done
well together.'

Charles nodded, but it looked as if his
thoughts were very far away. 'So to marry Miss
Parker you would go into the army again?'

'If I have to. I would have to leave someone to look after Hilltop, though.'

'You don't mean me?' Charles said, obviously aghast.

'Who else? You know the estate as well as I do and you care about it as much.'

'But—I can't run an estate! I don't know about farming and such.'

'You know as much as I do. We can learn together.' He suddenly realised how very concerned Charles had looked as he mentioned Helen. More than the concern of an old friend, mayhap? 'Or you could marry an heiress.'

Charles gave a humourless laugh. 'I doubt she would have me. You know I will help you however I can, though. No one deserves to find happiness as much as you, Harry.'

'I hoped you would say that.'

'Now you must persuade Miss Parker to marry you.' Charles smiled, a true smile this time. 'That poor lady.'

Harry laughed. 'I'm going to ride over to Hilltop this morning and fetch Mother's ring. Then we shall see.' He finished his breakfast and called for his horse, more filled with hope than he had ever been before.

'Miss Parker, are you unwell?' Lady Eleanor asked in a worried little voice. She went to Rose's side, where Rose was looking out the window of the nursery to the drive below, and slipped her small hand into Rose's. 'You look sad.'

Rose gave the little girl a smile that she hoped looked merry and reassuring, hiding the melancholy thoughts that invaded her mind. 'Not at all. I think I just danced too late last night and am now tired.'

Eleanor sighed. She looked so much like Jane in that moment it made Rose laugh. 'That's why Mama and Aunt Emma said they can't be disturbed until this afternoon.'

Rose laughed again. 'Too much Christmas will do that, I'm afraid.' She thought of her own Christmas, the night that meant she would never be the same again. She was a fallen woman and yet she did not feel 'fallen' in the least—she wanted to do it all over again. The one thing she knew could never be.

She glanced out the window, where she had seen Harry ride away from Barton only moments ago. Was he leaving for good? She had not been able to see his face, to read his expression.

Part of her feared never to see him again more than anything. And part of her was terrified of seeing him again. What would she say? What would she do? She was sure to make a fool out of herself no matter what happened. She had been unable to sleep at all last night when the dance was over, staring into the darkness of her bedroom, going over every single moment of her time with Harry, savouring every kiss, every touch, so she would always remember it.

It had made her feel so giddy with happiness. Being a fallen woman felt so wonderful that she wasn't surprised everyone preached against it so strenuously! If every lady knew how good it was, they would be clamouring to fall. She did not regret it.

But in the clear, cold light of day there was also a terrible sadness. Her time with Harry, even time just to see him or talk with him, was growing ever shorter. How could she steel herself to give that up? To go back to what she'd had before? Even knowing that she loved him and that she would always carry that love even if it was a secret in the deepest chamber of her heart.

Yet she knew that her love was exactly *why* she had to give him up. He needed so much more in his life than she could give him. He needed a fortune for his home, a society lady for his name. She would never have those.

'Shall we practise some of your music?' she said to Eleanor. She smiled down at the girl, trying not to think too much about how she would miss the children. How much joy they had brought her in her time with them. How lovely it would be to have her own little ones to teach music to, listen to their childish laughter and shrieks as they played their nursery games.

'It's Boxing Day!' William cried. 'Surely we deserve one day to play with our new toys.' He pushed his little carriage across the carpet, running it much faster than she hoped he would do eventually in real life. The others gathered close by, with their new dolls and tops and hoops.

'I'd like to play the pianoforte, Miss Parker,' Eleanor said. Rose smiled and led her over to the instrument where all their new sheet music was scattered.

'What would you like to play, then?' Rose asked. 'Whatever is your choice.'

'Something quite happy,' Eleanor said. 'I want to play something jolly while Mama gives out the gifts.'

Rose sorted through the songs until she found one she thought might suit, a lively reel that was well within Eleanor's skills. 'Perhaps this one? It's a bit harder than what we have tried so far, but you have made so much progress I'm sure you can play it very well indeed.'

'Oh, yes, I'm sure I can!' Eleanor exclaimed, her eyes shining with new confidence. 'Who will teach me once you leave, Miss Parker?'

Rose hugged her close, trying not to cry. 'I'm sure your mother will find you an excellent teacher, one much better than me.'

'But it won't be the same,' Eleanor whispered.

'Must you go, then, Miss Parker?' William said, forgetting about his carriage for the moment. 'We like *you* teaching us music.'

Rose bit her lip against those threatening tears. It would never do to cry in front of them, not on Boxing Day. 'And I love teaching you, very much. But I already have a job I must do.'

Eleanor wrinkled her little nose. 'With Aunt Sylvia?'

Rose nodded, trying not to contrast the reality of life with her aunt and the dream she had known last night. That way could only lie sorrow and regret, and she wanted none of those. 'Yes, with Aunt Sylvia. She needs my help just as you do.'

'But what if you had another job?' Eleanor said. 'Something where you could stay with us?'

Rose hugged the little girl close. 'I would like that so much. Yet sometimes I think life does not arrange things as we would like.'

Eleanor frowned. 'Then maybe life needs persuasion.'

Rose laughed. 'Maybe. Yet for now we have music to practise. Your mama will be handing around the Boxing Day gifts very soon.'

The rest of the morning was spent most pleasantly, playing at the pianoforte and building castles out of a new set of blocks. Rose forgot her worries about the future, all her doubts, as she laughed with the children. All too soon, though, the nursemaid came to fetch them and get them ready to go downstairs.

Rose went to her own chamber to change her dress and tidy her hair. As she put on one of her sensible frocks, a pale grey trimmed with blue, she glimpsed her lovely ballgown draped over the chair where she had left it last night. She picked it up and held it carefully, as if it might shatter as easily as the dreams she had let herself grasp all too briefly. The silk felt cool and light in her hands. She carefully folded it and tucked it into her travelling trunk. She might never wear it again, but she would always keep it.

She found her shawl and wrapped it over her shoulders, glancing in the looking glance to make sure her hair was neatly pinned. Luckily she showed little sign of her late night except some faint shadows under her eyes and paler than usual cheeks. She looked as she always did—practical, sensible Rose.

She left her chamber to make her way downstairs for tea with the other guests. She could hear Jane presenting the Barton servants with their gifts in the library and the sound of happy laughter. Rose knew that then the staff would depart for their day off and everyone at Barton would have tea and a cold supper, and then perhaps cards or charades. One more burst of merriment before the winter set in.

And tomorrow—tomorrow she would probably leave with Aunt Sylvia and the Barton Christmas would be only a memory.

Rose smiled despite the sad pang of such thoughts. It would only be a memory, yes, but what a grand one! She had never expected to have such a time in her life at all. It had been the best holiday gift.

She started down the stairs, which were deserted. Everyone seemed to be gathered in the drawing room or the library, not hurrying about as they usually were. But at the foot of the stairs she found she was not alone after all. Harry was in the hall, pacing back and forth, his brow furrowed as if he was in deep thought. She almost missed her step as she saw him, looking so handsome and strong in the daylight, and clutched at the banister.

Rose had thought she would encounter him

again in a crowd, where they would have no chance of a private word and where she could prepare herself beforehand. Where, if she was lucky and her acting skills were up to the challenge, she could just keep smiling and remain composed.

Now she had no chance to prepare herself at all. He glanced up and saw her there, staring at him open-mouthed like a starry-eyed, besotted schoolgirl.

She snapped her mouth shut and tried to smile carelessly, as if she did this sort of thing all the time. She remembered Lady Fallon, her perfect, half-bored mask, and tried to copy it.

She feared it was a terrible failure. So many emotions were flooding through her, all the things she had pressed down so hard for so many years, racing free. Hope, joy, laughter, despair. And she feared it all showed on her face.

'Rose,' he said, his voice eager as he made his way to the foot of the stairs. 'I've been waiting for you.'

'Have you?' Rose forced herself to keep walking down the stairs, holding tight to the gilded banister as if it could keep her from turning and fleeing back to her chamber. 'I've been at lessons with the children.'

'We have to talk,' he said.

Rose swallowed hard past a throat gone suddenly dry. Her stomach gave a nervous flutter. 'Yes, I know.'

'Shall we…?' He gestured towards the door to the small sitting room where they had first kissed.

She didn't want to be alone with him there, as she remembered all too well what had happened the last time. Close to him there, in the half-light, she was afraid she couldn't resist him again. Yet she knew there was nowhere else they could be alone. She nodded and hurried into the room ahead of him before she could indeed turn and run away.

Once she was alone with him there, she knew it was a mistake. He was too close, too warm, the smell of him all around her. She longed to throw her arms around him and never let go.

She sat down on the sofa and tightly folded her hands in her lap.

'Rose, I—' he began, then broke off with

a wry laugh, shaking his head. 'I fear I am no good at such things.'

Such things as breaking her heart? No, he had never done that. She had done it to herself, reaching for what she knew could never be hers. 'Oh, Harry,' she said. 'You need not say anything at all, I promise. I know how things must be. I would never presume anything, or cause your life any trouble. We part as good friends, always.'

'Part?' he said, frowning. He sat down beside her and reached for her hand. She dared to let him, dared to feel his touch one more time. 'Rose, no. That isn't what I want at all.'

She was confused, half-hoping for—what? She didn't even know. 'Then—what do you want?'

He smiled and squeezed her hand. 'I told you I am terrible at this sort of thing. I really should have read some of those romantic novels Jane has scattered around, but there was no time.' He reached inside his coat and took out a tiny box.

As Rose watched, unable to breathe at all, he opened it to reveal a beautiful ring, a round ruby surrounded by tiny pearls. It gleamed and twinkled at her, enticing her with all it promised.

'Rose, will you do me the great honour of agreeing to be my wife?' he said, a small smile hovering around his lips. But his voice sounded uncertain. 'I know I have little to offer you, but you would have a home at Hilltop and there would be the income when I return to the army…'

'The army?' Rose gasped. To go back to battle, when he had already nearly died there? 'No, Harry, you can't do that. Hilltop needs you and I've seen how much you love your home. You belong *there* now.'

'I do love it. That is why I will return to my commission. To earn what I can.'

'And that is why I can't let you do this.' Rose reached out and gently closed the box, unable to look at it any longer without being tempted. Tempted to throw her better judgement to the winds and run into his arms. 'Your duty is to restore your home and I have no fortune to help you do that. I have nothing to offer you at all.'

He shook his head. 'Rose, you know that is not true. You have yourself. You're the kindest, bravest lady I have ever known. I need you by my side. And after what happened last night…'

'I won't use that to tie you down to something you will come to regret,' she protested. 'You cannot go back into the army. You must find a wife who can be all that you deserve and it's not me. You would despise me one day.'

'I never could do that!' he protested vehemently. His hand tightened on hers. 'Rose, please. I need *you*.'

Unable to bear being close to him a moment longer without giving in, she snatched away her hand and jumped to her feet. 'Please, Harry, I can't be the anchor that ties you down. I—I care about you too much.' She bit her tongue to keep from blurting out what she really wanted to say—that she loved him. She loved him with a force and fire she had never believed was possible. And that was why she had to let him go.

Before she could change her mind, she threw open the sitting room door and ran out. The laughter from the drawing room was even louder now, but she knew she couldn't go in there yet. Not until she could compose herself. Half-blinded by tears, she dashed up the stairs to her chamber.

At the top of the staircase, she dared to glance back. Harry stood in the sitting room doorway, watching her with a desolate look on his face. She had not expected that, that he would want her to stay with him, and it broke her heart all over again.

She forced herself to turn away and walk to her bedchamber. Only once she was alone did she let herself fall to the floor, and cry out all her sadness and regret.

'What are you doing, Eleanor? Nanny will be so angry if she sees you there, when we're supposed to go downstairs soon,' William said.

'Hush!' Eleanor hissed at her brother. One could always trust William to ruin a covert session of eavesdropping. And without eavesdropping, how would she ever learn anything? Grown-ups never told children anything interesting. She pressed her ear closer to the door of Miss Parker's chamber and waved her brother closer.

He sat down on the floor beside her. 'What's happening?' he whispered.

'Poor Miss Parker is crying,' Eleanor whispered back. Her stomach ached in a most strange fashion, she felt so sorry for kind Miss Parker. The lady's sobs, even muffled by the door, sounded like the saddest thing Eleanor had ever heard. When she had peeked out the nursery door earlier, she had seen Captain St George standing in the hall while Miss Parker ran from him. She didn't know what it meant, but she knew they were both sorrowful.

William looked just as appalled. 'But what's wrong? Is she ill?'

'I don't know,' Eleanor answered. 'But I heard one of the housemaids say she thought she heard that Miss Parker had turned down a proposal of marriage. Could it have been from Captain St George? Can you imagine that?' To Eleanor, with her love of fairy-tale castles where handsome princes saved beautiful princesses with a kiss, turning away from romance seemed unthinkable. Especially if it made Miss Parker so unhappy.

'A proposal?' William scoffed. 'You girls are so silly about such things.'

Eleanor scowled at him. 'You just wait until *you're* grown-up and have to find your own countess! It won't seem so silly then. And anyway, surely Miss Parker loves the Captain or she wouldn't be sad.'

'That's true.' William gently pressed his hand to the door, as if Miss Parker could feel their concern even through the stout wood. Eleanor placed hers next to his. 'Why do you think she turned him away, then?'

'I'm not sure. I think it has to do with money.'

'Money?'

'Miss Parker has to teach us music, doesn't she? And she has to live with that old lady. And Mama says Hilltop has a roof that is falling in.'

'But that's silly. If just a roof is keeping them from getting married…'

'Yes,' Eleanor said thoughtfully. She did so adore Miss Parker, who loved music and was always patient and smiling, and never dismissed their ideas just because they were children. She liked the Captain, too, who was just like the brave, wounded princes in her stories. Surely they were meant to be together?

Surely they just needed a fairy godmother, one who could fix their roof and help them live happily ever after?

'William,' she said with excitement. 'I have an idea. Will you help me?'

'Is it for Miss Parker?'

'Yes. If we could find the lost treasure at Uncle David's estate…'

William's eyes widened as he grinned. 'We could get Uncle David and Aunt Emma to give it to Miss Parker and she and the Captain could fix their roof and marry!'

'Exactly. And then she would live next door to Barton and never leave us.'

'But where will we start?'

Eleanor frowned. 'In Papa's library, I suppose. There are lots of old maps there, maybe one could help us narrow it down.'

'We could go out after dinner tonight, when they're all in the drawing room. The gardeners always leave their shovels in the sheds at night.'

'We'll need lanterns…'

'What on earth are you children doing?' a sudden bark interrupted them.

Frightened, they leaped to their feet and spun

around. They found themselves face to face with Aunt Sylvia, who blocked their escape at the end of the corridor, all towering plumed turban, layers of fur-trimmed shawls and a most ominous dragon-headed walking stick.

William and Eleanor clutched hands. 'N-nothing at all, Aunt Sylvia,' William said. 'We were just…'

'On our way to lessons,' Eleanor said when he faltered.

'This is not your schoolroom,' Aunt Sylvia said. 'Isn't that the door to Miss Parker's chamber?'

Eleanor gulped and nodded.

'Then why are you lurking out here?' Aunt Sylvia demanded.

'We thought she might need some help,' Eleanor answered.

'Help?' Aunt Sylvia glanced at the door with a scowl. 'I see. Well, run along now. You should be doing your lessons, not pestering Miss Parker.'

Eleanor and William dashed away, hand in hand. 'Remember,' she whispered quickly when they saw the nursemaid looking for them. 'Tonight we look for the treasure.'

* * *

Sylvia impatiently pounded at Rose's door. She hadn't seen the girl for hours and she couldn't find the book she wanted. Rose always knew where to find things.

But, worse than that, Sylvia had seen Captain St George striding off down Barton's drive, his face like a thundercloud. She knew the look of heartbreak and profound disappointment on a man's face. Hadn't she caused such a thing herself more than once, when she was young and beautiful and careless in France? Those *affaires de coeur* had passed as quickly as a rainstorm.

But Sylvia had a deep suspicion that whatever was happening with Rose and Captain St George was nothing like that.

'Rose, I insist you open this door,' she called out sternly.

After a long, silent moment, the door swung open. Rose stood there, composed but pale, her eyes red-rimmed. 'How can I help you, Aunt Sylvia?' she asked.

'Oh, my dear girl. I think that for once it is how *I* can help *you*.'

Rose's mouth parted on a startled 'oh' and

Sylvia realised with a pang what an old crank she had truly become. She stepped into the room and shut the door behind her. She then did something she had never dreamed she could—she took Rose into her arms and held her close.

'Now, my dear girl,' she said. 'Tell me what is amiss.'

Chapter Seventeen

Helen tried to pretend that it mattered not a whit to her that Charles had not appeared for Boxing Day tea. Neither had Miss Parker or Harry, or a few others who were obviously still recovering from last night's ball. But it was Charles's face Helen searched for every time the drawing-room door opened and her heart sank every time she saw it was not him.

She feared her disappointment would show on her face. That her reputation as the scandalous, fun-loving, careless Lady Fallon would be ruined if she was seen actually to care for someone.

Care for someone. What a very strange idea, a new feeling. Rather like an ague coming on, making her feel feverish and restless and giddy. She hadn't felt that way in so long. Perhaps—never. And over a mere kiss.

A kiss from Charles St George, of all people. But, yes, there it was. She wanted to see Charles again, had to see him again. Had to know if what had happened meant anything at all to him, as it had changed everything for her.

She jumped up from the sofa and went to pour herself more tea, unable to sit still any longer. Jane and Emma sat by the fireplace, Jane embroidering and Emma with a book in her lap, talking quietly while everyone else played at cards or backgammon. It was a lazy afternoon with the servants gone, everything quiet after last night's ball. A few snowflakes drifted past the window, closing them into their own cosy world as the winter weather turned colder. Yet Helen felt filled with a sparking nervous energy.

She took a sip of tea as she gazed out the window at the bare trees of the park, the lacy haze of snowflakes. She remembered Charles's kiss, how it felt on her lips, the way his touch made her feel so very—alive.

She had come to Barton half-hoping she

could find something with Harry again, could recapture a bit of that girl she had once been, before Fallon and her whole shallow London life. She had only found that Harry, as brave and kind as he was, had never been for her. If they had indeed married when they were young, they would have been unhappy because they could never have understood each other.

But Charles—he saw who she *really* was, because he was the same. Seeking, restless, longing for something more.

As she lifted her teacup again, she suddenly glimpsed a figure in the grey gloom outside. Startled that anyone would have stayed out in the cold weather, she peered closer and saw to her shock that it was Charles, heading towards the house.

He wore his many-caped greatcoat, a scarf wound around up to his chin, and a hat pulled over his brow, but she knew it was him. Under his arm was tucked a leather-covered sketchbook.

Helen hurried from the drawing room, ignoring the curious looks that followed her, and found Charles handing over his winter wraps to a footman in the hall. To her surprise, he was smiling, his cheeks red from the cold, as light and merry as the Charles she had once known.

'What on earth were you doing out there?' she demanded. 'It's starting to snow. You could have made yourself ill.'

He just laughed. A *real* laugh, the kind she had not heard from him in so long.

'Would you have nursed me most tirelessly, Helen?' he said lightly. 'Brought me beef tea and bathed my feverish brow?'

Helen planted her hands on her hips. 'Certainly not. You brought it on yourself. What were you doing out there?'

'Sketching, of course.'

'Sketching? But—I thought you had given up art?'

'Yes. I saw this astonishing view when we were out sledding a few days ago, and well— I just had to capture it.'

He opened his sketchbook, and showed Helen a scene of the winter woods, looking out over the fields to the chimneys of Hilltop beyond. It was rough, hastily drawn in quick lines, but it was exquisite. The melancholy beauty of the view was all there, the chill winter emptiness with the hope of spring to come, the promise of new life.

'Charlie, I…' she began, but words failed her. She shook her head. 'It is breathtaking.'

He shrugged. 'Just a rough sketch. When I can procure some paints, I'll really be able to do something with it. If I could just capture the layers of white in the snow. That blue undertone, not quite grey, but not azure, either. I might have lost my touch.'

'Never. It was always there, just waiting for you.' Helen flipped through the rest of the pages. Most of them were still empty, but a few held the beginnings of sketches. A tenant's little girl with her doll outside a cottage. The summerhouse in the Barton garden.

She turned a page and found that she faced—herself. A profile, a small smile on her lips, her hair waving from her brow. A smaller view of her whole figure, sad and solitary against the terrace balustrade.

Charles snatched the book back and snapped it closed. Suddenly all that sunny openness, the wonderful enthusiasm he showed over his new art, was gone.

'Charlie, I…' she stammered. 'Do you see me that way?'

He shook his head. 'You know you are beautiful, Helen. Men must tell you that every day.'

'But you are different! That sketch makes me look so—lonely.'

'And so you are. You always have been, but you have also always been strong. If you would just believe me, Helen. If you would only see yourself as I always have.' He took up her hand and pressed a quick kiss to her fingertips.

'Oh, Charlie, you are strong, too! Your talent, the way you see the world around you— it is something no one else has. If you would let me help you…'

'No one can help me, Helen,' he said starkly, turning away.

'At least let me try! Let *us* try.' She had never begged anyone for anything before, but now she wanted to. She wanted to grab his hand, to hold him with her, to beg him to show her the world as he saw it.

He smiled at her, but it was sad, quickly gone. 'Helen, you deserve so very much more than what I could give you. I've never known a lady like you, a lady with all the potential of the world inside of her. Let me do the only right thing I've ever done in my life. Forget about me and live all your dreams.'

He walked away from her, disappearing up the stairs as she watched. She had never felt so bereft before, so hollow. So—alone.

'How dare you, Charles St George?' she whispered. She had offered him everything, wanted everything with him, and he had left her there alone.

Blast him, she thought. She wiped at her eyes and tilted her head high before she marched back into the drawing room. He was right. She did have everything. She was Lady Fallon, after all.

And Charles St George would be very sorry he ever dared to break her heart.

Chapter Eighteen

'Oh, Miss Parker! Something terrible has happened and I don't know what to do.'

Rose glanced up from the book she was pretending to read in the Barton library and saw the children's nursemaid standing in the doorway, tears streaming down her cheeks and her hands twisting in her white apron. It was raining outside, a steady, icy mist, and Rose had pleaded a headache when Jane took the other guests into the village for a musicale at the assembly rooms. Rose had hoped for a quiet evening to hide from her worries—and from seeing Harry, as he and Charles had left for Hilltop. She felt quite drained after confiding in Aunt Sylvia.

But it seemed her hopes for quiet were in vain. The tears in the maid's eyes made her own worry spring to life. She put down her book and hurried over to the girl. 'Whatever is amiss?'

'I went to look in on the children, as it's nearly their bedtime, and Lady Eleanor and Lord William are gone!'

'Gone?' Rose suddenly shivered with a cold fear. 'Are you quite sure? Perhaps they're just playing with their new toys in the day nursery. Eleanor was so determined to practise that new song…'

'Oh, no, Miss Parker. I looked there first thing. The younger ones were all asleep in their beds, but Lady Eleanor and Lord William are nowhere to be found. Their beds are still made, but I did find this.' She held out a rumpled sheet of paper.

Rose recognised it as a drawing by William, who was quite good at sketching and had been talking with Charles a few days ago about his sketchbook. It was a lady, a princess to judge by her tiara, standing by a large open chest of gold coins. The Princess held up her hands, as if beseeching someone to find her. At the bottom was scrawled, *Please don't worry, Miss Parker. We will help you. Don't leave us.*

Rose bit back a sob. 'Oh, my darlings, no,' she whispered.

'Do you know where they are, Miss Parker?' the maid asked.

'Perhaps, but I'm not really sure.' She made herself take a deep breath, to think quickly about what might be in their dear, fanciful minds. 'Send a footman with a message to Lord and Lady Ramsay, but do not alarm them too much. Say Lady Eleanor has a slight disposition. Tell her all when she arrives home. I think I might have an idea where they are and I'll go out to look for them.'

'Alone, Miss Parker?' the maid cried. 'In this weather?'

'There's no one else to go right now. Don't worry, I'll be quite well and I can move quickly on my own.' She wasn't at all sure about that, but she put as much confidence in her voice as she could. Panic would not help them now. 'Can you find me a lantern?'

She hurried up to her chamber and put on her stoutest boots and her hooded cloak. She only prayed she was right and that for some reason they had gone off to look for the treasure.

She left the house and was immediately tempted to turn around as cold, icy rain stung her cheeks. She knew she had to go forward, though. The children needed her. Harry would be brave in just such a situation; she had to take inspiration from him now. Hoping against hope that her lamp would not go out, she set off into the night.

The rain let up enough that she could just see the path in front of her, but the wind was icy-cold, biting through her cloak. She found the stone wall that divided Barton from David and Emma's Rose Hill and then led off at an angle towards Hilltop. That was where the children had pointed out to her the remains of the cold castle.

Rose carefully clambered over the wall and rushed towards where the ruined towers rose up in the misty night. The blank windows seemed to watch her dispassionately, completely unexcited after all the turmoil and trouble they had seen over the centuries. But were they a refuge as well, a place that would shelter two children?

The ground around the ruins was a quagmire of frost and mud, and Rose picked her way carefully closer. She glanced up at the column of what had once been a chimney, the bricks now tumbling down. Rose wondered for an instant what the house must once have looked like, all pale stone and shining windows, a refuge from civil war for two fleeing lovers. How had the long-gone lady felt when she hid her treasure, hoping to reunite with her love and find a new life together?

She had a fleeting image of Harry in her mind, his smile, his hand held out to her, helping her find strength, just as those lost lovers once had. 'Are you there?' she called out.

'Help!' someone cried, a tiny, faraway sound.

Rose spun around, her heart pounding. 'Eleanor? Is that you? Where are you?'

Oh, let it be the children, she silently pleaded. Let it not be Arabella's ghost, if there was such a thing.

'Help!' the voice cried again. A very real voice, a little girl, full of fear and desperation, but blessedly real.

'Eleanor? Where are you?' she called back, scanning the ruins with desperate eyes. She could only see the fallen chimneys, hear the whine of the icy wind. 'Can you hear me? It's Miss Parker!'

'Oh, Miss Parker! We're down here.'

Rose's heart pounded even harder as a rush of panic seized her. She hadn't heard William at all. 'Down where, my dears? Keep talking so I can find you.'

'Down here, under the stones. We fell through some boards.' Eleanor started singing 'I Saw Three Ships' in a wavering, heartbreakingly brave little voice.

Rose followed the sound until she found an old caved-in area that must have once been some kind of cellar. She could hear Eleanor's voice floating up from the depths.

She knelt down at the edge of the splintered wood, holding her lantern high. It flickered alarmingly. 'Eleanor, are you there? I can't see you.'

'It's—it's dark. We only have one candle,' Eleanor said, her voice thick with tears. 'And William hurt himself when we fell.'

Hurt himself? Rose sucked in a breath. She forced herself to stay calm as she said, 'Just move towards my voice, darling. All will be well now. I'm here.'

She heard the sound of tiny footsteps, the scrape of stones moving. 'Why on earth did you come out here on such a terrible night? You gave us such a fright.'

'We—we just wanted to help you.'

'Help *me*?'

'Yes. To find some money so you can marry Captain St George and fix his roof at Hilltop.'

'Oh, my darlings,' Rose said, trying not break into tears. 'You are truly the best of friends to worry about me like that. But you should never have put yourselves in danger.'

'But you love him! You have to be together. Like in the stories.'

'We can't worry about that right now.' She held the lantern higher and at last glimpsed a pale little face below. Eleanor blinked at the sudden rush of light. She had a scrape on her dirty cheek and the sleeve of her pelisse was torn, but other than that she seemed well.

'Oh, Miss Parker,' she sobbed. 'I'm so sorry.'

'It's all right, my dear. I'm here to help you

now. See that large stone over there? Can you climb up on it and reach for my hand?'

Eleanor nodded and clambered up on the fallen stone to reach up her small hand. Rose was able to grasp it and used all her strength to pull the little girl upwards. Her shoulder burned, but Eleanor was soon on solid ground next to her. Eleanor hugged Rose around the waist, her face buried in Rose's cloak, sobs shaking her tiny body. Rose held her tightly in return.

'What happened to William?' she asked urgently. 'Is he awake?'

'I think he hurt his arm,' Eleanor said. 'But he's awake.'

'Very good. Now, my dear, I need you to be very brave. A heroine princess, in fact,' Rose said, holding the girl's face between her hands. She hated to send her off, but she could think of no other way to quickly summon the needed help. 'You must run straight home and get help for your brother. Take the lantern and stay only on the path. I will climb down and stay with him until you return.'

Eleanor gulped hard and nodded. 'What if he…?'

Rose firmly shook her head. 'He will be fine. This is what you must do for him now. I know you can, I know how smart and brave you are. You are the smartest girl I know.' She handed Eleanor the lantern and gave her one more hug. 'Now run, as fast as you can.'

Eleanor dashed away. Once the bobbing lantern light disappeared into the mist, Rose took a deep breath and steeled herself to do what she must. She thought of Harry and his braveness in battle, and it gave her courage, too. She grasped the edge of the pit, its jagged wooden edges biting into her palms through her gloves, and eased herself down carefully until her feet touched the dirt floor of the old cellar. For an instant, everything looked blurry, then she realised her spectacles had been knocked askew. She pushed them up her nose.

The tiny, flickering light of the children's one candle showed her where William sat, propped up against a wall of rotting old shelves that still held dusty bottles of wine. He sat on a faded blanket and beside him was a small pile of yellowed parchment maps and a pair of shovels. They had not come unprepared.

Thankfully, he was also awake, his eyes wide open. But he held his right arm tightly with his left hand and his cheeks were damp with tears.

And the candle was burning quite low. They didn't have much time left.

'What happened, William dear?' she asked as she hurried to kneel beside him.

'I—I fell. My arm…' He gasped.

'I see that.' Rose carefully examined the arm and saw it was luckily not broken. She feared, however, that perhaps his collarbone was fractured. She wished she had some laudanum or brandy, but there was nothing. She could only hope Eleanor was very quick.

She tore a wide strip of linen from the hem of her chemise and used it to bind William's arm close to his side. She wrapped her cloak around them both and held him near, keeping a close watch on the sputtering candle.

'We just didn't want you to leave, Miss Parker,' he whispered.

'What do you mean leave, my dear? We'll always be friends, I promise.'

'We thought if you married Captain St George and stayed at Hilltop, you could still teach us music, and tell us stories,' he said.

'Oh, William. I will always help you, no matter where I live,' Rose answered, her heart aching.

'But if you love Captain St George…'

'Sometimes love isn't quite enough,' she murmured.

'Of course it is! What of the stories you told us? About warrior knights and their fine ladies? The Captain is a warrior knight.'

'So he is.' The bravest warrior knight she had ever known. But before she could say any more, William let out a shout. Rose heard the crack of a falling stone. There was a sudden, sharp, piercing stab at the back of her head. Dizziness and pain, as well as a terrible cold, overwhelmed her as she fell to the floor. She heard William yelling, but it seemed to come from very far away.

'Harry,' she whispered. Then everything faded to blackness.

Chapter Nineteen

'Captain St George!' Harry heard a little girl's cries just as he swung down from the saddle and handed the reins to a waiting groom at Barton. He had gone to Hilltop to put his mother's ring back in storage, but he had not been able to do it.

It was still in his pocket as he went for a long ride, long after the light faded and he should have returned to Barton. But he needed the movement and speed, the cold wind on his face, trying to leave behind thoughts of Rose. Memories of how she looked after he kissed her, the way it felt to hold her close. The pain when she turned him away. But she could not be outrun.

He only forgot his heartache now, though, as he heard a panicked cry. His battle instincts went up and he whirled around, reaching for a sword that was no longer there. He saw little Lady Eleanor running towards him, her face smudged with dirt and her jacket torn.

He reached out to catch her as she hurtled towards him. 'What is it, child? Are you hurt?' He studied her swiftly, scanning for wounds as he once did in the chaos of a battlefield, but there didn't seem to be any blood or broken bones. She did, however, look terrified.

Lady Eleanor shook her head and gulped in a breath. 'No, but—our parents have gone to the village, and—and you must come with me! At once!'

'No, we need to get you inside and send for the doctor. You can tell me about it once you're in from the cold.'

'We do need the doctor, but not for me,' Eleanor wailed. 'It's my brother and Miss Parker. We fell down into the ruins of the old castle and William hurt his arm, and she came after us, but I don't know what's happened now.'

Harry froze with fear. Rose had run after

the children into the freezing night, gone into the old ruins? But then his instincts took over and his mind because as clear as ice. 'You, there!' he called back to the groom. 'Who is still in the house tonight?'

The young man looked quite confused, as panicked children were probably not usually part of his job, but he answered quickly, 'Just the butler and housekeeper, sir, and perhaps the nursemaid and another footman. Everyone else has gone for Boxing Day and the family is in the village.'

'Then send for the nursemaid at once and bring as many men as you can find to follow me. We must go to…' Harry turned to Eleanor. 'Where is Rose, exactly?'

'The ruins of the old castle on Uncle David's land,' Eleanor said. 'In some old cellar. We fell in and couldn't get out.'

'Send the men after me to Rose Hill, with blankets and medical supplies,' Harry told the footman. 'And fetch a doctor at once.'

'Will they be all right?' Eleanor asked.

Harry hugged her quickly. 'I am sure they will be. Miss Parker is a most sensible lady.'

He took back his horse and galloped off

towards Rose Hill. He had to make himself focus, to stay in the cold mindset that had taken him through so many battles. It was more important now than ever. Rose needed him.

He couldn't, wouldn't, ever let her down.

Rose felt as if she was sinking down into the dark waves of some warm sea, drifting deeper and deeper. She knew she had to fight against it, to push herself up into the cold world again, even though she only wanted to sleep.

But there *was* something there, something she had to battle against no matter what. If only she could remember....

Then, with a jolt, she *did* remember. She was in the old ruins, she had gone there looking for the children and something had fallen on her. She could smell the damp, earthy scent of rotting wood and darkness pressed around her. How long had she been there? She could hear a sob, seemingly from very far away, and she remembered William was with her.

She drew in a deep breath and pushed herself into a sitting position. Pain shot through her head like a bolt of lightning and she feared she would be sick. She ground her teeth against the nausea and waited for the dizziness to pass before she took stock of her surroundings.

The children's candle had burned down to a tiny stub, but it still gave a little light. She saw the old, collapsing shelves that had long ago held wine bottles, the children's shovels and the rock where she had pulled Eleanor up. Very high up, she could see a bit of the night sky and even a star or two as the mist seemed to be lifting. Surely Eleanor would be back soon. She tried not to think of the little girl alone out there.

'Oh, Miss Parker, you're awake,' William sobbed.

'Yes, my dear. I'm awake.' She shivered and drew her cloak closer around them both. She closed her eyes and thought of Harry, imagining him there with her. Holding her close, keeping her warm and safe...

'Rose! Are you there?' he shouted, and for a moment she was sure it was just part of her dream. But then it came again, so loud and strong she knew it was real. 'Rose! Please answer me.'

'We're here,' she called back hoarsely. 'Can you hear me?'

His face appeared above her, blotting out the stars, the most beautiful sight she had ever seen.

'Are you hurt, my love?' he said.

'I hit my head. I'm afraid I fainted for a moment. Poor William's shoulder is hurt. Is Eleanor…?'

'She is safe back at Barton. The doctor and some of the servants should soon be on their way. Don't worry, I'll have you both out in only a moment.' He vanished again and after a moment she did indeed hear the murmur of other voices. A rope was lowered and Harry climbed down it with a swift power and grace that quite astonished her. He did look like a warrior prince, just as the children had said, coming to their rescue.

He knelt down beside them and helped William into a makeshift sling with a blanket and the rope. The boy was quickly drawn up out of their prison.

Rose feared she would burst into tears

as Harry gently took her into his arms. She clung to him, knowing at last that she was not alone. That she was truly safe. She rested her head on his shoulder and closed her eyes, all the pain and fear vanishing. It was just like in those sweet moments after they made love, all the worry and care of life gone perfectly quiet.

How could she ever give that, give *him*, up again? She clung close to him, feeling their moments together slip away.

'Let me help you up, Rose,' he said. 'You're safe now, I promise.'

'I know I am. With you.'

'Then why did you leave me?'

'Because you deserve more than a poor companion as your wife. You deserve—everything.'

'Oh, my dear.' He pressed an ardent, tender kiss to her forehead. 'You are all I have ever dreamed of wanting. You are so kind and sweet, so strong. And I am sorry, but I won't let you leave me again, not unless it's because you truly do not love me.'

'I do love you,' Rose said, her throat tight with tears. 'So very much!'

His arms tightened around her. 'Then it's settled. We are staying together. Nothing else will ever hurt you again, my dear, sweet Rose. Not when I am here. Because I love you, too.'

She was half-afraid to hope, even as his words thrilled her to her very soul. She had hoped for things before and seen them shattered, just as her family had cracked upon her father's death and their separation. Did she dare reach out now for her heart's desire and hold on to it, no matter what?

'What—what are you saying, Harry?' she whispered.

'I'm saying I've never been happier in all my life than when I am with you. I never even thought feelings like this were real. You show me that being alive can be a joy, a wonder! I never realised before you that I was only in some grey half-world, driven by some sense of dry duty. Now I see what there can truly be.' He looked deep into her eyes, not letting her turn away. Not letting her run again. 'Please, do not send me back to that. Say you will be my wife.'

How very, very tempted she was, how

filled with raw, burning longing. 'But—what will we do?'

'I could go back into the army, or learn how to be a farmer—a real farmer, who could make Hilltop profitable again. You need have no fear that I will take care of you and that we will make a true home of Hilltop. It may not be exciting or glamorous…'

'But we will take care of each other,' Rose said. She at last let her tears flow free, her emotions fly out into the world. 'I knew that day with you at Hilltop that I wanted to belong there, with you. If you want me, then I am yours, and I'll do anything I can for our life together.'

Harry laughed, a glorious sound full of a sheer joy she had never heard from him before, but which she hoped to hear again. But now perhaps she *would* hear it, again and again, every day of the life they would build together. She hardly dared believe it was true.

'Please, Rose,' he said. 'Say you will marry me. I can do anything if you are beside me.'

And she knew she could do anything with him. He was the best man she had ever met, brave and kind and strong. 'Yes, Harry St George. I will marry you.'

He smiled, like a burst of sunlight in the dank old cellar, and he reached into his coat to retrieve the box he had once offered her. 'It's fortunate I didn't lock this away again.' He opened it to reveal the ruby and pearl ring, shining and beautiful, full of promise. 'I know my mother would want you to have it.'

'Oh, Harry,' she whispered. She could say nothing else. Her hand trembled as he slipped it on to her finger. It shimmered there, like hope itself.

He lowered his lips to hers for a lingering kiss—just as they heard a clamour from the world outside. A shout, the sound of their names being called.

'It seems we must now be rescued,' Harry said.

Rose laughed. 'I must say, I am very glad they waited for us after all.'

Chapter Twenty

'Are you sure you feel quite well, Rose?' Emma Marton asked as she arranged a tea tray on Rose's bedside table. 'The children are begging every five minutes to see you, but the doctor said you must rest...'

'I am very well indeed, Emma,' Rose answered. 'The doctor just left for his second visit and he says I may even come down to dinner. My head is quite well. I have missed the children.' She had also very much missed seeing—and kissing—Harry, who had only been allowed in for a quick word that morning. She knew the days of Christmas were still going on downstairs, and she didn't want to miss a minute.

'And they miss you. They are so terribly sorry for what they did.'

'They were only trying to help. They have such good hearts.'

Emma sighed. 'I know. It does get them into trouble sometimes. Bea and I once found ourselves in the same predicament before David and I married. David boarded up the old ruins, but now he says he will fill them in altogether.' She paused to rearrange a vase of greenery on the table. 'I understand we are to have a happier event here at Barton quite soon, though!'

'I hope so. Lily's husband has gone himself to beg a special licence from the archbishop.'

'A Christmastime wedding! How lovely.'

'Yes. I think it will be. Jane says she is bringing in even more greenery to deck the drawing room.'

'Everyone does love a romance here!' Emma said with a laugh. 'When I came back to Barton after I was widowed, I was so tired, so heartsick. I never imagined I would find someone like David here. And Barton helped Jane and Hayden find their way back to each other, too.' A soft smile lit her face. 'There is magic here. Something that brings hearts together, when they are meant to be.'

Rose laughed. 'So it does. This has truly been the most wondrous Christmas.'

'And now we shall all be neighbours!' Emma said, clapping her hands in delight. 'What do you and Harry plan to do at Hilltop now?'

'I am not sure.' She frowned as a worry pierced through her happiness, the fear that Harry would indeed go back into the army. 'There is so much to start on. I think Lily will stay and help me for a while.' As a curate's wife, Lily was well practised in making a lovely house on economies, but still Rose worried. She wanted to make everything so perfect for Harry, for their new life together.

'Well, I am glad you will be nearby. What fun we will all have together!'

As she clapped her hands again, the chamber door opened and Jane appeared with her arms overflowing with silks, satins and laces. 'I thought we might like to look through these, Rose,' she said, draping the gowns over chairs and the end of the bed, a shimmering rainbow. 'There's no time to have something from the dressmaker, of course, but Emma and I are quite handy with our needles. We could make over a few of these. Perhaps the lace from this gown on that blue silk?'

'I was going to wear my dress from the Christmas ball,' Rose said. She reached out to gently touch the blue silk, as soft and light as a cloud, and as pale as ice. Surely Harry would think she looked pretty in that! 'But this one is so lovely…'

'It will be perfect!' Jane said. 'And Lily says she had heard from your mother this morning and she should arrive later today and will bring her old wedding veil with her.'

'Mama is coming?' Rose cried. She had feared there would be no time for her mother to arrive and now the day would be perfect.

'Yes. It's meant to be a surprise, I'm afraid,' Jane said. 'Hayden has sent his fastest horses and carriage for her.'

There was the faint sound of wheels crunching on the frosty gravel of the drive below Rose's window. 'Maybe that's Mrs Parker now,' Emma said, glancing outside.

A puzzled frown creased her brow. 'No, it's a carriage I don't know. And Aunt Sylvia is waiting down there.'

'What?' Rose and Jane cried. They hurried over to peer past Emma's shoulder. Aunt Sylvia did indeed wait on the front steps, swathed in her shawls, leaning on her walking stick. She looked a most formidable figure, but Rose now knew the kind heart that truly lurked beneath. She had listened to Rose when she dared not confide in anyone else.

The carriage, a plain but respectable and well-kept barouche, rolled to a stop and a man in a dark coat and hat stepped out, a leather case under his arm. Aunt Sylvia took his arm and they vanished into the house.

'How odd,' Rose murmured. She and Aunt Sylvia had had a long conversation after the doctor left, about Rose's forthcoming marriage and her former life with Aunt Sylvia. Sylvia had seemed rather out of sorts, as usual, and declared that no one could read aloud as Rose did, yet she had also talked of hiring the local vicar's youngest girl as a companion, as if she had already made the plans.

'Do you know the man, Rose?' Emma asked.

'I think I have seen him before, but I'm not sure,' Rose said. 'Aunt Sylvia does often have her men of business call, but I rarely meet them.'

Jane laughed. 'Men of business do rather tend to look alike. Hayden said Mrs Pemberton had quite commandeered his library this morning. Ah, well. We have important things to discuss ourselves. Such as—will Eleanor be allowed to be your attendant? She has made herself quite sick for begging the honour...'

That evening, Rose made her careful way downstairs before dinner. She still ached in places she had not even realised she possessed muscles after her adventure in the ruins, but the doctor said she could be out of bed for a few hours. Eleanor and William insisted on helping her, holding on to her hands. They had begged her forgiveness for running off and been thoroughly hugged and forgiven.

And waiting for her in the hall was Harry. She remembered seeing him there after she first turned away his proposal, but tonight he looked quite different—younger, his features lit with a smile. He held out his hand to her as she reached the last step and drew her close.

Rose went into his arms with joy and he lowered his head to kiss her. Eleanor sighed, while William made a dismissive snort.

'Girls and romance…*ew*!' he gasped.

'I told you, William—just you wait until you are grown,' Eleanor said. 'Then you will understand.'

Rose and Harry laughed, holding tightly to each other. But there was no time for another kiss, as Aunt Sylvia appeared at the library door and banged her stick on the floor.

'You are not married yet, Rose,' she said. 'You have not yet stolen her from me, Captain St George. I would appreciate a word with you both for a moment.'

William and Eleanor fled from her frown, and Rose exchanged a long glance with Harry. He shrugged and offered her his arm and they followed Aunt Sylvia into the library.

The gentleman who had arrived so mysteriously earlier that day sat at the desk, papers and ledgers stacked before him. He glanced at them over his spectacles and nodded.

'Rose, you remember my lawyer, Mr Rodd,' Aunt Sylvia said, sitting down behind the desk. 'Mr Rodd, this is Miss Parker's intended, Captain St George.'

'How do you do,' Mr Rodd said. 'I must say what a fortunate pair you two are.'

Rose glanced up at Harry, who looked as puzzled as she felt herself. 'Fortunate, Mr Rodd?' Harry said.

'Indeed. Mrs Pemberton and I have just been going over the terms of her will, as well as a few current property deeds. This coal mine in Wales looks especially promising…'

Rose was now most confused. 'Coal mines?'

'And some farmland, as well as these London warehouses,' Mr Rodd said. 'Mrs Pemberton has made them over to you, effective after your marriage. If you could just sign here, Captain St George…'

'Wait a moment, Mr Rodd,' Harry said. 'Mrs Pemberton, what does this mean?'

'I am most fond of Rose, Captain St George,' Aunt Sylvia said gruffly. 'Very fond indeed. She has made my life quite a great deal brighter these last few years and I know very well I am not easy to live with. She is good girl and deserves whatever I can do to help her now. I have no children and these properties can't go with me to the hereafter, as old Pemberton found out when he left me a widow so long ago. You and your children might as well enjoy them. The leases will help Rose now and my whole estate will be hers when I am gone.'

'Oh, Aunt Sylvia,' Rose whispered. There had been so many lovely surprises in the last few days, she wasn't sure she could bear yet another. 'I had no idea you cared for me so.'

'Of course I do,' Aunt Sylvia said, waving her walking stick. 'You are a kind girl, Rose. I hope you deserve her, Captain St George, for I am loathe to let her go.'

'I don't think anyone is good enough to deserve Rose, Mrs Pemberton, least of all a man like myself,' Harry said. 'But this is too generous. We cannot accept.'

'Oh, pish!' Aunt Sylvia cried. She waved her stick again, forcing Mr Rodd to duck. 'You have no choice at all. It's already done. If you choose not to spend the income, it will accrue to your children. But I have to say, young man—if you do not allow me to make Rose's life a little bit easier now, I will be angry indeed. And you would not care to see me angry.'

Harry laughed. 'No, Mrs Pemberton, I would not. Nor would I ever do anything to hurt Rose. This will be her property to use as she wishes.'

As she wished! Rose thought of so many things—a roof for Hilltop, a new school, plenty of servants to see to the house's grand restoration, Harry able to carry out his improvements. Harry not being forced back into the army. She could hardly believe it. She rushed over to hug her aunt. 'Oh, Aunt Sylvia. How very kind you are.'

Aunt Sylvia awkwardly patted her shoulder. 'You of all people, Rose, know that is not true. I am not in the least kind. And I expect the best seat at your wedding, even if your silly mother *is* on her way to Barton.'

'Of course, Aunt Sylvia. I will even toss you my bouquet.'

Aunt Sylvia shuddered. 'No, my dear. Believe me, one marriage was quite enough.'

'So, Jane darling, do you plan to give up matchmaking now?' Hayden whispered to his wife as they sat in the Barton drawing room after dinner, watching Rose play at the pianoforte as Harry turned the pages of her music.

Jane tilted her head to study the lovely picture the two of them made, so glowing with happiness. 'I admit I misjudged what Harry needed in a wife,' she admitted. 'I quite forgot the important lesson I once learned from our own marriage. Love and friendship are the two most important things. With those, anything can be accomplished. I am happy they discovered that for themselves.'

'Then—no more matchmaking?' he said, clasping her gloved hand in his.

Jane glanced at Helen Fallon, who sat alone in the window seat. She glittered with emeralds, as beautiful as a young goddess—but her eyes shimmered with what looked terribly like tears.

'Well,' Jane murmured. 'It *would* be a shame to waste such valuable lessons in love, don't you think?'

Epilogue

'There! I think we have done quite a fine job here, don't you?' Lily said as she straightened the lace veil on Rose's curled hair. Once their mother had worn it, then Lily. Rose had never expected to don it herself.

'You have indeed,' she answered, studying herself in the looking glass. Her pale blue gown with its frothing lace train, the lace veil, the bouquet of winter greenery and white hot-house roses—it was all quite splendid. She could barely believe it *was* her. 'A silk purse.'

Lily laughed. 'You weren't exactly a sow's ear to start, my dearest sister,' she said. 'But shouldn't you take off your spectacles?'

Rose nudged them up her nose. 'I think I need to see the bridegroom.'

Lily laughed. 'Quite right.'

There was a knock at the door and Jane appeared. 'I think all is in readiness downstairs, Rose.'

Rose nodded, taking in a deep breath against the sudden nervous fluttering deep inside. 'I'm ready.'

She followed Jane and Lily to the top of the stairs, where Eleanor waited to scatter her flowers. The banister was twined with greenery and white ribbons, and she could hear music from the drawing room. It looked like a fine wedding indeed and Rose could hardly believe it was *her* wedding. That her own brave prince awaited her.

Jane and Lily disappeared into the drawing room and Rose followed the pathway of petals Eleanor laid for her. The drawing room, decorated with more blue and white ribbons and tall vases of flowers, was filled with people, including Mr Hewlitt in his cassock waiting to perform the ceremony, her mother sniffling into her handkerchief and Aunt Sylvia in her promised seat of honour. But Rose only saw the man who waited for her at the holly and ivy-wreathed altar. Her own Christmas bridegroom.

He smiled at her brilliantly, so tall and handsome in his blue coat. She smiled and hurried forward to take his hand, all nervousness forgotten, every doubt vanished. She was truly at home at last.

* * * * *

If you enjoyed this story, you won't want to miss these other great reads by Amanda McCabe

THE QUEEN'S CHRISTMAS SUMMONS
THE DEMURE MISS MANNING
BETRAYED BY HIS KISS

MILLS & BOON®

HISTORICAL

AWAKEN THE ROMANCE OF THE PAST

A sneak peek at next month's titles...

In stores from 30th November 2017:

- **A Secret Consequence for the Viscount** – Sophia James
- **Scandal at the Christmas Ball** – Marguerite Kaye *and* Bronwyn Scott
- **An Unlikely Debutante** – Laura Martin
- **Besieged and Betrothed** – Jenni Fletcher
- **Rescued by the Forbidden Rake** – Mary Brendan
- **The Rancher's Inconvenient Bride** – Carol Arens

Just can't wait?
Buy our books online before they hit the shops!
www.millsandboon.co.uk

Also available as eBooks.

MILLS & BOON®

EXCLUSIVE EXTRACT

Read on for a sneak preview of
A SECRET CONSEQUENCE FOR THE VISCOUNT
by Sophia James
the final book in the daring and decadent series
THE SOCIETY OF WICKED GENTLEMEN

'I was more than surprised to see you tonight. I don't know why you would wish for all those years of silence and no contact whatsoever, but—'

'It was not intentional, Lady Eleanor. My memory was lost.'

Her eyes widened at this truth and she swallowed, hard.

'I must have been hit over the head, as there was a sizeable lump there for a good time afterwards. As a result of the injury my memory was compromised.'

She now looked plainly shocked. 'How much of it exactly? How much did you lose?'

'Everything that happened to me before I disappeared was gone for many years. A month ago I retrieved most of my history but still…there are patches.'

'Patches?'

'The week before my disappearance and a few days after have gone entirely. I cannot seem to remember any of it.'

She turned at that, away from the moonlight so that all her face was in shadow. She seemed slighter than she had done a few hours earlier. Her hands trembled as she caught them together before her.

'Everything?'

'I am hoping it will come back, but...' He stopped, because he could not know if this was a permanent state or a temporary one.

'How was your cheek scarred?'

'Someone wants me dead. They have tried three times to kill me now and I doubt that will cease until I identify the perpetrators.'

'Why? Why should you be such a target?'

'I have lived in the shadows for a long time, even before I left England, and have any number of enemies. Some I can identify, but others I can't.'

'A lonely place to be in.'

'And a dangerous one.'

'You are different now, Lord Bromley.' She gave him those words quietly. 'More distant. A harder man. Almost unrecognisable.'

He laughed, the sound discordant, but here in the night there was a sense of honesty he had not felt in a long, long time. Even his friends had tiptoed around his new reality and tried to find the similarities with what had been before. Lady Eleanor did not attempt to be diplomatic at all as she had asked of his cheek and his circumstances and there was freedom in such truth.

He felt a pull towards her that was stronger than anything he had ever known before and stiffened, cursing beneath his breath.

DON'T MISS
SECRET CONSEQUENCE FOR THE VISCOUNT
BY SOPHIA JAMES

Available December 2017
www.millsandboon.co.uk

MILLS & BOON®

Why shop at millsandboon.co.uk?

Each year, thousands of romance readers find their perfect read at millsandboon.co.uk. That's because we're passionate about bringing you the very best romantic fiction. Here are some of the advantages of shopping at www.millsandboon.co.uk:

* **Get new books first**—you'll be able to buy your favourite books one month before they hit the shops

* **Get exclusive discounts**—you'll also be able to buy our specially created monthly collections, with up to 50% off the RRP

* **Find your favourite authors**—latest news, interviews and new releases for all your favourite authors and series on our website, plus ideas for what to try next

* **Join in**—once you've bought your favourite books, don't forget to register with us to rate, review and join in the discussions

Visit **www.millsandboon.co.uk** for all this and more today!